~AUTHOR ACKNOWLEDGMENT~

This book is dedicated to my late mother, who filled my life with love and happiness, and whose unfailing belief in my dreams helped them to come true.

~OTHER BOOKS~

by Lucille Naroian

Talk of the Town – This saucy and humorous romance involving a mystery writer and a celebrity talk-show host is available now at Amazon and other popular online book retailers.

Unforgettable – A softhearted playwright and spunky gal jilted at the altar go head to head in this emotional romance. Available now at Amazon and other popular online book retailers. (Read a short preview at the end of this book.)

DARK CRESCENDO

At the highly publicized funeral of her famous pianist husband, Joanna Reed Dalton unexpectedly sees her former lover, Nick Jordan, and is overwhelmed with yearning and unanswered questions.

Joanna's father, Boston physician Dr. Carlton Reed, hated Nick, a common construction worker, and tried to keep him from Joanna. Nick disappeared, seeming to give up on Joanna when she foolishly agreed to marry her Julliard piano instructor, Steven Dalton. During the entire three years of her loveless marriage to Steven, Joanna has longed for Nick – and now he's back in her life. But will he stay when Joanna's father tries to keep them apart once again?

Nick's obviously after something, but Joanna's not sure if it's romance or revenge. The truth of the past builds in a dark crescendo of danger and heartache that can't possibly end well – or can it? The final notes will ring true, heralding the death of a lost love, or a new beginning.

DARK CRESCENDO

by

Lucille Naroian

Licensed and produced by
Penumbra Publishing
www.penumbrapublishing.com

DARK
CRESCENDO

by

Lucille Naroian

CHAPTER ONE

*T*he peal of a lone church bell cut sharply into the early winter morning as a heavy rain fell on the throng of mourners filing into limousines outside the Church of the Good Shepherd.

In the candle-lit sanctuary, Joanna Reed Dalton stood tall and composed, her left hand resting lightly on her father's arm. Not once throughout the long, somber ritual did her clear blue eyes lift from the mahogany casket containing the remains of her husband, Steven Dalton.

To her friends, professional acquaintances, and the hundreds of fans who had come to pay their last respects to the world-renowned pianist and composer, the young widow's demeanor held all the restrained grief and dignity one expected from the mate of an Olympian god. However, no one, not even her father, knew the extent of blessed relief the maestro's untimely death had brought her.

* * * * *

When the service concluded, a slender, gray-haired sexton swung open the heavy wooden doors in the back of the church. Rain-swept wind rushed in, jolting Joanna to the reality of her surroundings. Shivering from the cold, she allowed her father, Dr. Carlton Reed, to pull her closer to him while the pallbearers slowly guided the bier down the wide granite steps and into the back of the hearse.

In the darkened, now empty church, Joanna and her father quickly made their way to the vestibule. Just as they approached the last pew, the bulky figure of a man stepped out of the gray shadows, blocking their passage. Gasping audibly, Joanna's eyes widened in shock at the sight of Nick Jordan, just as handsome and virile as she remembered. Her heart pounded wildly in her chest as his smoldering gaze caught and held hers. For one brief moment, it was as if the last three years without him had never been. He watched her intently, studying her surprised reaction to his unexpected appearance. Unable to sustain her composure, she felt her whole body go limp against her father.

"Son of a bitch," her father muttered, pulling Joanna close.

Nick moved in, his expression venomous as he glared at him. Her father scowled, his face flushed with fury. Joanna glanced from Nick to her father, wondering what was going on between them. Without a word, her father abruptly pulled her past Nick and guided her from the church toward the waiting limousine.

Unable to stop herself, she glanced furtively over her shoulder to catch a last glimpse of the man she'd given up three years ago, to marry the man she was now burying. But Nick was nowhere to be seen, and all that was left for her was the casket carrying the remains of the man now gone from her life – forever. The overwhelming pain of loss squeezed her chest, making her gasp before she finally turned and got into the limousine.

After putting up with Steven for what seemed an eternity, his death meant nothing to her ... except freedom. It was the pain of giving up *Nick* and being without him that cut through her heart like a knife every time she thought about him. And seeing him now made the shock even harder to bear. She expected time to ease the intensity of her feelings for him, but it didn't. Sitting next to her father in the back seat of the limo, she could barely contain her tears.

The winter rain pounded heavily on the funeral procession as the line of black cars rolled at a slow, even pace on the three-mile journey to the cemetery. Biting her quivering lower lip, Joanna settled her body against the limousine door, glancing out the rain-blurred window to avoid a possible confrontation with her father. Right now, she was in no mood to talk to him, nor did she want him to see her tear-stained face. She knew she couldn't fool him into believing she was crying for her dead husband.

Without a word, her father dropped his handkerchief onto her lap. She lifted it to her face, then darted a quick glance at him. His dark eyes blazed, but he remained silent, refusing to answer her unspoken question. Someday she would get him to tell her why, after so many years, Nick Jordan still had the power to arouse such fierce emotion within him. Someday ... but not now.

She turned back to the tinted window and concentrated on the rivulets of rain streaming down, blurring the world outside. Inevitably, her thoughts returned to Nick. She wondered again where he'd been, and what he'd been doing for the last three years – and why he'd showed up at her husband's funeral. After Steven's accident, her housekeeper Louisa had mentioned offhandedly that she'd heard Nick was back in Boston again. But Joanna had been too wrapped up in the confusion of Steven's death to pursue the issue then. Now she wondered ... was Nick married, with a couple of kids? Perhaps divorced? Could he still be interested in her? Maybe that's why he'd showed up at the church – to try once again to rekindle their relationship.

She bit her lower lip hard to stop that torturous line of thought. How could he still be interested in her, when she'd been married three years to another man, especially given the tone of their last meeting? She hadn't heard from him or seen him since that night – until today. Sighing heavily, she told herself now was not the time for thoughts like that. She had a husband to bury. Later, after this was all over, she could lose herself in the familiar fantasy of being with Nick

Jordan once again. Only this time perhaps her forbidden private fantasy could actually become reality...

* * * * *

The wind howled around the car, driving the rain down on the mourners hastily making their way to the green canvas canopy, beneath which rested the flower-laden coffin. When Joanna's limousine stopped at the base of the gravesite, an usher quickly pulled open her door, struggling to steady a large black umbrella against the gale-force wind. Slowly Joanna glanced over her shoulder, casting a sorrowful look at her father scanning the rolling hills of the cemetery. For a moment her grief for the dead was genuine. As a young teenager, she had come with her father to this very place to bury her mother.

Her father lifted his collar to shield his face from the pounding rain, then stepped beneath the umbrella. He wrapped his arm around her shoulders, offering protective support as they made their way to the gravesite.

Just as he had eleven years before, her uncle, Monsignor Daniel Reed, awaited them beneath the scant shelter of the canopy. Only now she was not a young girl of fourteen experiencing the trauma of losing her mother, but a woman of twenty-five, a celebrity in her own right, who had come to bury her husband.

With head bowed, Joanna glanced tearfully at him, quickly remembering how the tall, yet gentle priest had tried repeatedly to persuade her to cancel her wedding to Steven, positive she had not given full thought to the difficulties in dealing with a temperamental celebrity twice her age. Little did he know it was his brother – her own father – who had pressured her to marry the famous Steven Dalton and abandon the man she truly loved.

"Come, Joanna," her uncle said softly. He lowered his head and placed a light kiss on her forehead, then pulled her closer and whispered something, but she was too distracted to acknowledge what he said as she scanned the crowd again, hoping to catch a glimpse of Nick. Unable to spot him, she chastised herself for her girlish and inappropriate foolishness. Dutifully she fixed her eyes on the spread of roses that flanked the coffin as her uncle moved away and addressed those gathered for the service. She tried unsuccessfully to concentrate on the scripture her uncle was reading. Her eyes kept wandering, seeking out Nick Jordan, but seeing only an unrecognizable mass of mourners.

Just as the brief service came to an end, a piercing streak of lightning illuminated the dark sky, followed by a loud clap of thunder that jolted Joanna so severely, she almost pitched forward onto the casket. She wanted to run and hide the way she always did as a child whenever a thunderstorm loomed overhead, but she was rooted to the wet ground.

Within seconds, a group of hysterical girls began pushing their way through the crowd, nearly knocking Joanna down as they clawed at the casket, grabbing for a floral souvenir. Overcome with panic, Joanna turned to flee from the unruly mob, but a hand clutched the back of her black lace mantilla, ripping it from her head and nearly taking a lock of her dampened hair with it. She screamed in terror as she and her father became caught in the mob now surrounding them. Clamoring voices, together with the sound of clicking cameras, filled Joanna's ears as scores of reporters and television crewmen recorded the mêlée.

"Get me out of here! Please!" she cried, pressing her hands to her ears as she buried her face in her father's chest. The crowd refused to set her free, continuing to paw her, some thrusting cameras in her face. The cemetery was now a scene of pushing, clawing, scurrilous combatants caught up in a bizarre contest to touch her and strip the casket of its blanket of roses.

Joanna pushed through the mob, frantically seeking the security of the limousine. Just as she reached for the handle, the door flew open, and the chauffeur pushed her inside. Joanna fell onto the seat, sobbing hysterically, her disheveled hair matted against her face. Her father followed swiftly behind, locking the door angrily against the crowd. "Quickly, Jason!" he ordered, drawing Joanna into his arms.

CHAPTER TWO

*W*eaving in and out of the heavy downtown traffic, the chauffeur finally turned onto a quiet narrow lane and brought the car to a halt before the understated elegant edifice of a three-storied brick townhouse on Beacon Hill. Joanna considered it home; though, due to her and Steven's concert schedules, she spent less than six months a year there. Once inside the house, Joanna passed through the foyer and entered the spacious living room. Automatically kicking off her shoes, she flung her sopping-wet coat onto the white leather sofa that dominated the room.

"Really, Joanna," her father admonished, snatching up the dripping garment. "You ought to be more careful with the upholstery."

His chiding remark riled her, and she spun around in a rage. "Is that all you can say after what we've just been through? That I'll damage the furniture? To hell with the leather! To hell with everything! Those people at the cemetery acted as if they'd gone mad, groping and grabbing at the flowers – and clawing at *me* – like a pack of wild hyenas! Not to mention the press with their microphones and cameras. They turned Steven's funeral into a three-ring circus! I'm so furious, I could turn this room inside out. And *you* – you just–"

"Just *what*, Joanna?" Her father shot her a look, then moved swiftly past her.

She jutted her hands in the air. "You just shrug things off, no matter how awful they are!" She wanted to point out how coldhearted he sometimes could be, but figured there wasn't much use. He had been a brilliant surgeon who had to deal with success or disappointment on a daily basis, with the power of life or death in his gifted hands. Now, as head of the hospital's cardiac unit and commanding a seat on the board of directors, he held a different kind of power, but certainly his days were filled with strife and daily crises. She couldn't really blame him for developing the knack for distancing himself from the emotional fallout of things that happened around him.

Her father nodded his head but said nothing, indicating he understood her frustration and anger all too well. He went to her and gently gathered her in his arms. "Yes, it was terrible," he whispered, stroking her damp hair. "It was frightening, damn frightening. But you must remember that Steven was no ordinary man, and you, his widow, are no ordinary woman. Like it or not, what happened today was news, and the reporters were only doing their jobs. As for the crowd, well..."

Placing a tender kiss on her forehead, he affectionately lifted a strand of wet hair from her brow. "Why don't you take a nice relaxing bath, and I'll get Louisa to make some tea." He looked around inquisitively. "By the way, where is Louisa? And why wasn't she at the funeral?"

"She left early this morning," Joanna said as she slipped from his arms and walked toward the fireplace. "I asked her why she wouldn't be at the funeral, but she merely shrugged me off and said she had something more important to do."

After lighting a fire in the hearth, Joanna stepped back and began running her fingers through her matted hair, allowing her blond locks to loosen, separate, and cascade about her shoulders in damp and heavy ringlets. Her father stood at the bar, his back to her. His broad shoulders drooped slightly, the way they always did when he was tired. For Joanna, it was an indication his guard was down, and now was the moment to strike. "You knew there was tension between Louisa and Steven, didn't you?" she accused as he mixed a tall glass with scotch and water.

He hesitated, then admitted, "Yes."

"Then surely you know how long it had been going on."

He huffed impatiently. "Really, Joanna, must we play games with each other?"

"How long, Father?" she persisted. "I want to hear you say you knew *exactly* what was going on in this household since the first day Steven and I moved in here."

He gulped his drink and turned away from her,

obviously irritated. "I don't know why you keep harping on this subject, Joanna. What went on between you and your husband during your marriage is, frankly, none of my business!"

"It damn well is!" she bellowed. "You've spent a lot of time and energy seeing to it that my whole life is your business!"

"Joanna–"

The phone in the study rang, saving him from having to make an admission Joanna knew he'd rather avoid. He was very careful to skirt around the issue of Steven's many personal faults and indiscretions, as if purposely overlooking them would make them somehow not real.

Joanna cast her father a parting glare as she headed into the adjoining study to answer the phone. It didn't occur to her until she reached the desk that she might not want to answer any phone calls at this time. The ringing stopped. But it didn't stop the ringing in her memory. A ringing phone had brought all this to a head four days ago. A ringing phone had actually contributed to her husband's death.

She placed her chilled fingertips against her warm forehead as she looked at Steven's dark and quiet cell phone lying in the clear plastic zipper bag, along with his wallet, both collected from the wreckage. He'd been on the phone, talking to *that woman*, on his way to the airport to see *their daughter*, when his car had skidded off the rain-slicked road and slammed into the guardrail, killing him instantly.

DARK CRESCENDO   *Lucille Naroian*

With her chin trembling, she reached out and snatched up the bag, ripping it open to extract the phone. She flipped it open and turned it on. The low-battery warning beep went off as she scrolled through the menu icons to find his stored messages. There it was ... the message that had sent him tearing out of the house to get to the airport. *Steven, our daughter lies in critical condition in hospital. Terrible pool accident. Please come quickly. Love always, Yvonne.*

Joanna skewed her face in a scowl, thinking of Yvonne Martell, the famous mezzo-soprano opera star, who'd been Steven's secret lover for more than twenty years. She was also the mother of their seventeen-year-old daughter, who had been lying comatose in a California hospital. In an odd twist of fate, the woman who loved Steven Dalton had also contributed to his death.

Joanna flipped the phone closed and absently set it aside on the grand wooden desk where Steven liked to gather his paperwork and organize his thoughts with a pot of steaming tea. He'd also sit there for hours, talking privately on his phone to his beloved Yvonne.

Tears rolled uncontrollably down Joanna's face. When the call came, Steven had screamed at her to book the quickest flight to Los Angeles as he packed a few things. She'd been busy on the phone, trying to secure a seat for him on a seven o'clock flight, when he'd rushed out the door without so much as a goodbye. That was the last time she'd seen her husband alive.

She glanced out the darkened rain-streaked window behind the desk. The rain continued to pound outside, as if it intended to drown the whole world along with her sorrow ... sorrow for Steven's frustration and anger ... sorrow for the three years they'd wasted together, pretending for a fickle and unforgiving public that they were a happily married couple. And sorrow for what might have been, what could have been, and most of all, what *should* have been, had she made choices based on her heart instead of what others told her was the 'right thing to do.' She sucked in a shaky, sobbing breath as fresh tears slid down her cheeks.

The last time she'd seen Nick was at her and Steven's prenuptial party. It had been raining just like this. He was hurt and angry over her decision to marry Steven, and his sudden appearance that night had been as unexpected and unsettling as it had been today at Steven's funeral. She closed her eyes, reliving that night, going over the details in her mind ... details that she'd memorized like a recital piece. She could picture the sights, sounds, and scents as if she were actually there...

* * * * *

The elaborate chandeliers overhead cast glittering lights over the Plaza Hotel's grand ballroom. The delicious odors of expertly prepared food laid out in a dazzling display wafted through the air to entice the small crowd of formally dressed guests mingling about. Steven had carefully selected each and every person to attend and celebrate their upcoming union. As Joanna gazed across the small crowd of well-dressed guests, she realized nearly everyone was somehow connected with Steven professionally. Few of them were friends of hers, and that said something sad about her and her life. Among the guests was, of course, Joanna's father, a steady presence to oversee the festivities and ensure that everything went smoothly. He was never far from Steven's side, as if he were Steven's self-appointed private counselor and mentor.

Joanna had never looked lovelier, with her thick, honey-colored hair piled high on her head in a mass of ringlets dotted with seed pearls. Matching pearls adorned the strapless bodice of her ice-blue gown that accentuated her tall, slender form perfectly, and brought out the cool blue of her eyes. She pretended not to notice the admiring glances as she genially moved from one conversation to the next in her role as honored hostess. But, she couldn't say that she felt happy, despite the occasion being celebrated – her upcoming wedding. A dark void inside her reminded her constantly that happiness was not in the cards for her future. She'd spent the last four years punishing whatever piano keyboard was in front of her, as she tried without complete and lasting success to please the harsh taskmaster who would soon be her husband.

And before that, it had been her father she'd tried to please in exchange for affection and approval. She couldn't be sure which of them was the more exacting director of her life, but she knew she'd never again experience a moment of freedom and happiness, as she had when she was with Nick Jordan.

She quickly squashed all thoughts of the man who'd brought joy to her life and then slipped away like a thief in the night. Glancing in Steven's direction, she found him assuming his usual role as instructor, performer, and center of attention. His suave and cultured air, combined with fair hair and incredible good looks, gave him an overconfidence that could be stifling to those around him. He was certainly respected and revered, and his admiring fans loved him, but he was not necessarily liked by those who knew him well. Despite the fact that he was twenty years Joanna's senior, they were visually a perfect match – according to her father. Steven's ashen-blond hair, so pale that it appeared silver in the sunlight, blended into his smooth ivory complexion. But his piercing gray eyes hid secrets ... secrets about which Joanna had only vague suspicions at the time...

The guests had persuaded Steven and Joanna to honor them with a private duet. Steven had immediately agreed, and hesitantly Joanna had complied. Once they had taken their places at the twin pianos on the ballroom's dais, a hush fell over the group as the melodious strains of Beethoven's *Moonlight Sonata* filled the room. Joanna's hands had trembled slightly as they passed over the keys, and although technically she had made no error, her timing had been slightly off, and twice she failed to strike the notes with clarity.

Steven had caught the blunder both times, and, out of the corner of her eye, Joanna could see he was furious with her. She watched the color in his cheeks change from crimson to arctic white, intensifying her nervousness while his long, slim fingers glided precisely and effortlessly over the keys. Whenever her eyes encountered his, she stirred uncomfortably, hoping he would smile and put her at ease. Instead, the muscles in his face grew taut, and the arctic coldness in his eyes sent a chill down her spine.

Their audience, held spellbound by the haunting refrains of the melody, had been unaware of what was transpiring between them. So often Joanna had played the sonata with ease and self-assuredness, the melody seemed to end as quickly as it had begun. When the final notes were struck, cries of *Bravo! Encore! Encore!* exploded in the room. Steven, scanning the awestruck audience, came to his feet and took Joanna by the hand. Suddenly, his fingers tightened cruelly around hers, hinting at the greater harm he wished to do her. She heaved a dramatic sigh in an effort to calm herself.

When the ovation failed to subside, Steven took the microphone in his free hand and gallantly gestured toward Joanna. Refusing to look at him, the tears stinging at the back of her eyes, she continued to bow and smile at their guests. But inside, she wanted to run from the room, so completely overcome by the mixed feelings of humiliation and anger at his overreaction to a less than perfect performance. Dutifully, she had stood by his side as Steven spoke. "Ladies and gentlemen ... friends ... we wish to thank you kindly for your warm response, but I'm afraid the hour is late, and my bride-to-be is a bit weary. Isn't that right, darling?" The last word, said in a caressing tone, was belied by the mocking smile fixed on his lips. Taking her slight nod as agreement, he slipped his arm around her waist in a gesture of devotion for all the guests to see, then escorted her down the steps and onto the ballroom floor. Ordinarily she would have responded in kind to his flippant remark, but she had no desire to do battle with him in public, and it had taken all her self-control to murmur a polite *thank you* and *goodnight* to their departing guests. Her father, the last to leave, kissed her goodnight and left.

Alone with Steven, and no longer able to control her anger, she shouted, "What the hell's the matter with you?"

"There's nothing wrong with *me*, my love," he replied through clenched teeth. He turned his back on her and headed for the stage. He was purposely punishing and humiliating her for two undetectable flaws in her performance that no one else had even noticed. After stepping up onto the stage directly under the light, Steven turned. His face was beet red. He studied her for a moment, then demanded, "Get up here. Now!"

DARK CRESCENDO

Joanna had had enough of his moods and theatrics. She'd put up with it while they were on tour, but she wasn't about to endure it now. "No. I'm tired. I just want to go home!"

"I said, *get up here!*" he commanded, pounding his fist on the side of the piano.

Joanna jumped, startled. "What the hell is your problem *this* time?"

He ignored her question and merely said, "I want you to sit at the piano and play the *Moonlight Sonata* for me. Only this time, I expect it to be played the way I taught you!"

Joanna looked at his eyes, wild and fiery, and thought he surely had gone mad. Not wanting to provoke him further, she forced a smile and said, "All right, Steven, if that's what you want. But, won't you play it with me?" Choking on her words, certain he would refuse, she stared wide-eyed with surprise when his mouth turned slightly upward at the corners.

Forcing herself to meet Steven's stare, she waited breathlessly until he finally spoke. "Very well. Come in on the count of three."

She slowly approached the dais and settled herself at the piano, suddenly feeling as if she were trapped in some weird Twilight Zone episode, or maybe a nightmare from Hell. Over the course of their last tour together, Steven had become like a stranger, not the man she had come to know and admire. At one point, she'd convinced herself she could actually grow to love him, after he'd wooed her and proposed marriage. When, after the repeated urging of her father, she'd actually accepted Steven's proposal, he inexplicably changed his behavior toward her, as if the very idea of marrying her repulsed him. His fury and contempt, combined with her pre-marital jitters, made her fear that marrying a man with such a horrific temper would be a disastrous mistake, despite her father's insistence that Steven was likely the best choice of a marriage partner she would ever run across. And she couldn't debate that sage advice, after Nick Jordan had disappeared from her life without so much as a goodbye. His unexplained absence – after she'd called hospitals and done everything she could think of to track him down – still hurt her to the core. She felt abandoned ... and used. But still, his love seemed so genuine, so real. How could he make love to her with such tender ferocity, and profess his love to her over and over – and then just walk away?

She shut thoughts of Nick from her mind and concentrated on Steven's subtle signal to begin. Together they played as one, and this time Joanna met Steven note for note, without hesitancy or error. As they approached the final bars of the sonata, she noticed that the muscles in his face had begun to relax, and the color in his cheeks had returned to normal. Closing her eyes, she breathed easier, assured her perfect performance would mend the discord between them. The melody ended on a soft, sweet note, with Joanna's eyes meeting Steven's as their hands lifted slightly above the keyboard.

The slow and deliberate clapping of hands shattered the quiet in the empty ballroom.

"Who the hell...?" Steven shot up from his piano just as a man in a rain-soaked trench coat walked toward them.

Joanna gasped. "Nick!"

Steven's eyes flashed first to Joanna and then to the intruder. "Who are you, and what do you want?"

"Why don't you ask the lady who I am, Mr. Dalton?" Nick turned to Joanna. "She and I are far from strangers, aren't we *Miss* Reed?"

Joanna winced as Steven stepped toward her. He made no move to touch her, but went to the end of the stage and flipped the switch, throwing the ballroom into a blaze of multicolored lights.

Nick stepped up onto the luminous stage, then casually slid down on the seat next to Joanna. "Jordan's the name," he practically crooned. Joanna didn't move, but merely lifted her gown and pushed it aside to keep it from getting wet.

"Am I supposed to explode in a jealous rage just because you know my fiancée, Mr. Jordan?" Steven laughed, folding his arms across his chest as he leaned against the piano.

Turning toward Joanna, Nick slipped his strong, hard fingers over hers. She sat spellbound, unable to remove her hands from beneath his grip. "Your party was announced on the social page of today's paper," he said softly. "I had hoped you'd come to your senses and realize the horrendous mistake you'd be making by marrying this clown. I can't believe you put up with his bullshit tonight."

"Now, just a minute, Jordan!" Steven lunged to the edge of the piano.

"Shut up, Dalton!" Nick glared venomously at Steven. "Your phony charm doesn't impress me. You're nothing but a bully and a coldhearted bastard. You don't love Joanna. You couldn't possibly, and torment her the way you did tonight."

"Stop it, Nick!" Joanna pleaded. "It's not what you think. Steven meant no harm. It's just that–"

"It's just that he doesn't give a damn about you, and you know it." Nick looked her in the eyes, and she turned away, unable to face him as wild thoughts rushed through her mind. Where had he been for the last six months? Why hadn't he tried to contact her, at least to let her know he was all right?

"I'm surprised at you," he said in an accusing tone. "The fun-loving blond spitfire I know would never let herself be abused by a cocky bastard like this." His gaze traveled insolently down her body. "No. He certainly doesn't love you, and you don't love him either. I *know* you don't."

"Is that a fact, Jordan?" Steven quipped, his handsome features twisted in a smirk. "And what makes you so sure?"

"This." Nick unfastened the buttons on his coat. Joanna looked at Steven, as surprised as he appeared to be. Over the pounding in her ears, she heard Nick announce clearly, "Here's my proof!" She watched in disbelief as Nick unfolded two large copies of sheet music, badly crumpled with frayed edges. He placed them on the rest above the keyboard.

"That's it?" Steven queried, looking down at Nick with smiling eyes as he pointed to the papers with his long, elegant fingers. "Two pieces of sheet music? Surely this must be a joke." He chuckled smugly.

Joanna sprang to her feet, the scarf of her chiffon gown brushing against Nick's flushed cheek. "Where did you get these?" she cried out, yanking the papers from the piano and blushing under the cold surveillance of both men.

"Don't you remember?" Nick chided. "You wrote this song for me when you were still living in the dorm at Juilliard. Although you never finished it, I wanted it. I still want it." His voice was rough and dry as he reached for the music Joanna now held tightly to her breast. "But, most of all, *I still want you!* It's not too late to get away from this madman, Joanna. Come with me – right now!"

Her fingers parted at his touch, the sensation sending a tingle throughout her body. She didn't quite understand what was happening to her, but a feeling of sensuous frailness enveloped her.

Here before her stood two men – two very different men. One, a wealthy, famous musician who was about to make her his bride. The other, a common laborer, strong and powerful, who had professed – and showed – his desire for her above all others, and had come to win her back. Six months before, Nick had disappeared from her life without explanation, with no contact, leaving her powerless to do anything about it. Her father victoriously announced that Nick's behavior proved what a cowardly scoundrel he was – a man she should be glad was finally out of her life. She still suspected her father had somehow been behind Nick's disappearance, and she regretted her weakness in not standing up to him and confronting him about it. But Dr. Carlton Reed had always been a strong-willed, controlling man. And, for some reason, he couldn't stand the idea of Joanna being with Nick.

"Nick," she said softly, her eyes lowered in embarrassment, "You disappeared without a word. I tried to contact you, to find you, but you seemed to have dropped off the face of the earth! At one point, I thought ... something terrible ... had happened." She swallowed back the sudden urge to cry. Trembling, she sighed and tried to smooth her ragged emotions. "After six months, what else was I to think, but–"

"You're absolutely right," he admitted, closing his eyes for a moment. "I lost my job and couldn't find work..." He opened his eyes and stared hard at her. "But, things are better now. I'm here, and I desperately want you back." He slipped the papers back inside his coat pocket. "I was a bloody fool to ever let your father convince me I wasn't good enough for you."

"W-What?"

"I'm over that now. I'm back here, back home, to stay. And I want you to come with me, away from this pompous jerk who's old enough to be your father."

"Nick .... what did you say my father–"

"He called me trash, scum of the earth. He said there'd never be room in your life for someone as common as me. He had me convinced I'd never be able to give you the lifestyle you deserved, that I'd just drag you down with me. At the time, I was unemployed and couldn't find another job. The hardest part of it all was that I couldn't tell you – I was too ashamed. I was down on myself, and I started to believe what your father said – that I was worthless and that you deserved better. I actually thought I would be doing you a favor by letting your father pick your future husband – this fine and cultured professor here." Nick snorted. "I can see now how foolish I was to let anything your father said get to me."

Joanna sank to her seat. "Oh, Nick..." She sighed, eyeing him anxiously. "Why did you come here tonight – of all nights – with the scribblings of a starry-eyed girl?" She felt stupid for ever thinking she could write music of any consequence. She could play the piano, but she was no composer. And she certainly didn't have the experience to know what was best for her future. Her father had reminded her of that constantly, ever since she was a child. He'd kept repeating over and over that she was just as flighty and prone to silliness as her mother – and she knew how things turned out for *her*. A passionate woman who loved to have fun, her mother had enjoyed their little tea parties and taking her shopping. But gradually she changed. She argued more with Joanna's father, she cried constantly. She became fearful, accusing him of trying to poison her. And finally, she'd ended up institutionalized, dying alone in a psycho ward, ranting about her husband killing the only man she'd dared to truly love...

Joanna shook her head. She couldn't allow herself to end up the same way. She needed to follow a prescribed regimen of order and control. Those few months of wild abandon that she'd enjoyed with Nick were not how life really was. Her father had sternly reminded her that hard work, her nose to the grindstone, would keep her grounded in reality – and keep her sane. Work, her career, and responsibility would give her a sense of accomplishment and prevent her from going off the deep end, like her mother had. And he was also quick to point out that a man who'd love and leave her, as Nick had, would do it again.

Tears streamed down her face, and her words oozed as she whispered, "I-I can't, Nick. I've already promised to–"

"To what? To sacrifice yourself at the altar of this self-proclaimed god? Look at him, Joanna! Take a really good look at him! He's nothing but a vampire in a tuxedo. Give him six months, and he'll suck the life right out of you." He stopped and sighed deeply. Although he was talking to Joanna, he cast a mean look in Steven's direction. "Get rid of the guilt, sweetheart. You don't have to do anything you don't want to do. You love *me*, and we both know it! I can see it in your eyes."

She turned away, shaking her head and swiping at her eyes. "You don't know ... you don't understand. I *need* to do what's right, what's best for..."

"Do what's best for *us*, Joanna!" Nick grabbed her by the shoulders and forced her to face him. "I know right now I can't provide you with the fancy, expensive home and cars that you're accustomed to. And maybe I never will be able to. But what matters is that I love you. *I'll always love you!* And that's more than the famous Steven Dalton can ever say."

He pulled her close, not roughly, but tenderly, as though she were fragile and might break under his strong hands. When he pressed his cheek against hers, they both sighed heavily. His touch was strong and forceful, yet comforting, and she thrilled inwardly, knowing he had come to her in spite of everything and everyone. He loved her ... and, for one precious moment, nothing else seemed to matter.

It was Steven who finally broke the long, unending silence. Surprisingly, his voice was quiet and controlled. "Go with him, Joanna, if that's what you really think is best. I won't stop you. However, I don't intend to stand here and be a witness to this melodrama any longer." Grabbing his coat, he stepped down from the stage. "I'm going home," he said, his voice devoid of emotion. "Kindly afford me the common courtesy of a phone call when you get home tonight. I'm sure that Mr. Jordan will see that you get there safely. If the wedding is to be canceled, then it will need my immediate attention." He was out the door before Joanna was able to absorb the impact of what had just happened.

"Smart man, that Dalton," Nick said, grinning. His voice sounded confident and self-assured as he added, "He knows when he's been beat."

Tears clouded her eyes. "He hasn't been beaten, Nick. He knows I'm going to go through with this wedding. I have to. I can't cancel out. If I did, the fallout would be devastating. You don't understand, and I can't explain it to you right now. So let me go. I have to stop him!"

He turned his head away for a moment to collect himself, then turned back and faced her. The sad expression in his warm brown eyes was enough to make her heart break. "I'm beginning to get the picture," he said, softly. "It's your father, isn't it? He's the man I should be dealing with."

Joanna's tears slid uncontrollably down her cheeks as she watched Nick walk out of her life for the second – and last time.

* * * * *

Swiping at the tears dampening her face, Joanna shook herself free of that painful memory. Nick had been right. Her father had everything to do with it. He'd seen to it, from the time she was a child, that she had no confidence, no self-esteem. She lived in a

constant state of fear. She'd driven Nick away in fear
... fear that she couldn't handle happiness ... fear that
she couldn't live life without her father's constant
guidance and approval ... fear that if she chose a
happy life married to a man she loved, the prize
would be failure and disaster. She couldn't handle that
– at least not then.

But now, after three years of living the lie of a
marriage in name only, of surviving constant
loneliness and mental abuse from a cruel man who
hated the very sight of her ... now she realized she was
a lot stronger than her father gave her credit for being.
She had lived without Nick for three long, tortuous
years, and now she was *free*. Free to live life her way,
good or bad. Free to love the only man she'd ever
wanted.

She straightened and turned toward the study
door standing ajar, affording her an unhindered view
of her father in the living room. She watched him fix a
drink and take a long, leisurely swallow. He sighed
with apparent satisfaction, seeming content with
himself, as usual. He suffered no fears or self-doubts.
Everything he did was done with surety of purpose
and conviction.

Nodding to herself, she moved forward to
confront him. It was time to take his lead and operate
with the same self-confidence. It was time for him to
pay for the hurt and misery he'd made his family
endure, as far back as she could remember. But most
of all, it was time for the worm to turn.

CHAPTER THREE

"*Louisa's* finally come home," Joanna announced, hearing the woman's car pull into the driveway. She turned from her father and looked out the window. "Poor soul. She looks exhausted."

"Serves her right," her father snapped. "It's hardly a day to be gallivanting about. And if I know her, she'll be wanting a sympathetic ear. Well, she won't get one from me."

Anxiously Joanna turned and faced her father. "You're angry with her? Why?"

He looked reflective, as if he could see in his mind a scene he was sure had taken place. "I think your devoted housekeeper has paid a call to that obnoxious Nick Jordan."

Joanna's eyes widened at his startling remark. If her father had intended to shock her, he succeeded. But Joanna refused to allow him the satisfaction of seeing how much his revelation had affected her. He was up to his old tricks again, she told herself. He knew the mere mention of Nick's name would send her emotions soaring to the surface.

Joanna hurried across the spacious room to open

the door and welcome Louisa home. But her father was at her side by the time she reached the entrance to the foyer. "Wait here," he demanded coldly. He swung open the door.

In her usual curt manner, Louisa announced, "I went shopping."

"Obviously," he quipped, scanning the array of wet packages piled high in her saturated shopping bag. "Come inside quickly, and take off those hideous galoshes. They're dripping puddles on the floor."

Without a word, she set her bag down and removed her rubber boots. When she reached the closet, Joanna's father grabbed the wet handle of the shopping bag. "I see your shopping expedition was extremely fruitful," he announced in a brusque tone. "It must have taken you hours to select your purchases."

Joanna watched in irritation as her father's knuckles turned white from the pressure his fingers were exerting on the bag handle as Louisa tried to pull the bag free. "Let go, you old fool," Louisa ordered in a tone just above a whisper. "The handle's ready to tear."

"I'm not the fool you think I am," he countered. "I'm guessing you've paid a visit to that man I don't need to identify."

Louisa's head jerked up. "I don't know what you're talking about."

Joanna's father raised his eyebrows, "You know *exactly* what I'm talking about. Nick Jordan. His presence at the church this morning was no coincidence."

Louisa snorted. "He didn't need to learn about the time of the funeral from me. It was no deep, dark secret; it was printed in the newspapers!"

Joanna advanced toward them, stopping whatever her father was about to say to her housekeeper. "Louisa, you're dripping wet," she said softly. "Why don't you put your rain slicker in the closet and sit by the fire to warm up?"

Her father frowned, and Joanna thought their bantering had ended, until he turned back to Louisa and snarled, "There's no doubt in my mind that you made personal contact with him. It appalls me to know that a member of this household has betrayed me."

Louisa's eyes flashed wide. "Betrayed *you*? I'm not going to stand here another minute and give account to you for my actions! My loyalty is to your daughter, not to you!"

Joanna stood immobile, stunned as her father pushed his face dangerously close to Louisa's. "I'm well aware that you disliked my late son-in-law, but his death does not give you free reign to usher Nick Jordan back into the picture, which is what I'm sure you were planning. If you value your position here, I suggest you keep to your duties and mind your own business before –"

"Joanna's happiness *is* my business!"

"How dare you! You are a servant in this house,

and nothing more!" The hardness of his voice plus the cruelty of his words brought tears to Louisa's eyes.

"*Father!*" Joanna bit out savagely, astounded at his verbal assault on her housekeeper. The older woman, trembling now in the grip of emotion, turned and stormed into the kitchen.

Shuddering with sudden anger, Joanna glared at her father. "You have no right intimidating Louisa that way!"

"She is a *servant*, Joanna. I was merely putting her in her place."

"I will not tolerate your insulting her. *I* pay her salary, not you. And she is much more than a servant. She is like family to me."

A sinister grin crept to her father's mouth. "She's more than that, Joanna. She's your cohort. I wouldn't put it past you to have persuaded her to go to Jordan this morning. I saw the way you looked at him in the church, and frankly, it disgusted me."

Joanna reared back, appalled by his attitude. She still had no clue after three years why he hated Nick Jordan so intensely. "It's your evil mind that torments you, Father. It's turned you into a cruel and heartless man. And if you don't apologize to Louisa, I'll never forgive you." She hesitated a moment expecting a rebuttal. When none came, she turned away from him and entered the kitchen, slamming the door behind her.

Louisa was looking for her apron in the lower cabinet, and when she found it, she brought it out with shaky fingers. She had obvious difficulty securing it around her thick waist.

Joanna embraced her warmly. "Calm down, Louisa. You know Father. He didn't mean to chastise you so harshly. It's just that his nerves are rubbed raw by the funeral and that chaos at the cemetery. Of course, seeing Nick at the church didn't help matters." She peered into Louisa's eyes, trying to reassure her.

Louisa shook her head. "I'm afraid this time I've overstepped my bounds. Your father has just cause to react the way he did. I should have left well enough alone."

Joanna stared at her anxiously. "So it *is* true? You really did go to see Nick this morning?"

"Yes." Louisa frowned and lowered her head in shame.

"Whatever made you do such a thing?"

"I only wanted to see if-" She caught herself and bit her lip. "It was an impulsive act, and I'm sorry I did it. I should've known your father would have guessed where I went. He was right, and look at the trouble I've caused." Feeling dejected, she dropped down onto a nearby chair. "The saddest part is ... nothing good will come of it."

Joanna ignored the pounding of her heart and refused to let her mind be distracted by thoughts of Nick. She had to concentrate on what Louisa was saying. Was she trying to tell her something? "What do you mean? Nick came to the church. I saw him. He made his presence there quite obvious to me."

Louisa seemed to struggle for the right words. "But ... it doesn't mean–"

"What's going on in here?" Joanna's father snapped as he pushed through the door in a huff.

Joanna turned on him, annoyed at the intrusion. "Nothing is going on!"

"Well, if the two of you can tear yourselves away from each other for a minute, I'd like some coffee." He glanced toward Louisa and softened his tone slightly as he added, "That is, if it wouldn't be too much trouble." He then turned and left the room as quickly as he had entered.

Louisa reached to the cabinet above her and began taking down cups and saucers. "Joanna, why don't you change your clothes while I brew the coffee? We'll talk later."

* * * * *

By the time Joanna descended the long spiral staircase and entered the living room, Louisa had set a serving tray with hot coffee and sweet rolls on the glass coffee table. Dressed in a long apricot-colored robe, with her hair secured at the nape with a matching ribbon, Joanna curled up on the loveseat, tucking her bare feet under her. Louisa and her father sat on the sofa arranged in an L-shape next to the loveseat. They were engaged in quiet conversation, and Joanna hoped the discord between them was over. Apparently it was, as Louisa turned to him and asked calmly, "Would you like me to turn on the television? It's time for the afternoon news."

He nodded, then poured steaming coffee into the delicate china cups. Reaching out, he handed a cup and saucer to Joanna. She put the cup to her lips and commented with a smile, "This smells wonderful."

Instead of acknowledging her comment, he scowled at the large flat-panel screen. Joanna glanced toward the TV and saw a video-taped replay of Steven's funeral. She grabbed the remote and turned up the volume. The voice of an off-screen news reporter narrated the details of the event, while a camera scanned the burial sight, zooming in on a tall, dark-haired man who stood leaning against a silver Lincoln Continental. Joanna's eyes moistened as she glanced quickly at her father – he saw him too.

"That's enough of that," her father announced, reaching for the remote control.

"Don't you dare turn it off!" she protested, maintaining her grip on the remote.

"Joanna, there's no point in reliving that disastrous event again. Look how unnerved you've become. And why not? The sight of Nick Jordan is enough to unnerve even the most stable person."

Louisa set her coffee cup down with a nervous clatter as the camera's view moved back to the reporter, with a background shot of Steven's coffin behind him. Joanna stiffened. The reporter looked into the camera and said, as if he were speaking directly to her, "This is the second time this week that tragedy has struck the music world. On Sunday, the daughter of mezzo-soprano, Yvonne Martell, succumbed to head injuries received in a fall at her Los Angeles home. She was seventeen years old."

Frozen in place, Joanna startled from her trance only when her father grabbed the remote control from her hand and turned off the TV. In the sudden silence, she stared unseeing at the blackened screen. The beat of her heart accelerated rapidly, and a sense of excitement filled her. The replay of her husband's funeral was the last thing on her mind – all she could think about was the fact that Nick Jordan had been there. Then she remembered – that was what her uncle had tried to tell her at the cemetery.

"Forget about seeing him, Joanna," her father warned. "I won't have it." She glanced sidelong at him as he raised an eyebrow with his signature touch of arrogance.

Joanna pressed a hand to her face, feeling the rise of color invade her cheeks. "I don't know what you're talking about."

"Come now! You are so transparent, I can almost read your thoughts."

"I was thinking no such thing!" The statement was a lie, but she wasn't about to admit it. "In any case, you have no business telling me what I can or cannot do!"

"You're *not* to see him!" her father repeated, raising his voice.

Before she had a chance to refute him, he stepped

away from the seating area and announced curtly, "I have to check on surgery schedules at the hospital. But, before I go, let me remind you, in case you've forgotten. You are now the widow of world-renowned maestro, Steven Dalton, and you will conduct yourself as such, with dignity and respect." He lowered his head and surveyed her intently. "All social activities are to stop. Do you understand?"

Joanna was stunned by that ultimatum, and it took her a second to find her tongue. "I *won't* have you telling me–"

"You *will!*" he commanded. "You will do exactly as I say." He walked to the foyer closet and took his coat, then headed for the door.

Frozen in anger, Joanna sat in teary-eyed frustration for a moment, then lunged up from the loveseat and ran after her father. By the time she reached the door, her father had already stepped outside and closed the door behind him. She opened the door and screamed into the darkness, "I'm a grown woman, and I'll do exactly as I please! Steven's no longer here to make my life miserable, and I'll be damned if I'll let you continue where he left off! Mind your own business, Father!"

She saw the taillights of the limo heading down the driveway in the rain-soaked night and slammed the door shut. Leaning back against the door, she banged her clenched fists against it. "Damn him!" she growled, breathing hard as her head pounded. *I let my chance for happiness slip away once, but I won't do it again!*

I'm free of Steven now – free to finally live my life. And no one's going to screw things up for me. Not my father ... not anyone!

Wiping away her tears, she turned and saw Louisa standing beside the hall closet, patiently waiting for her to regain her composure. She sucked in a deep breath and exhaled harshly. "I'm sorry for making such a scene," she said, walking toward Louisa, "but I seem to be at the mercy of my emotions today."

"Quite understandable, dear," Louisa said softly. She linked an arm around Joanna's and walked with her toward the spiral staircase.

Joanna sighed, feeling suddenly exhausted and relieved. They were alone in the house now. They hadn't had a moment's peace since Steven's death, and the silence of the huge, stately townhouse prompted Joanna to finally relax. Wearily she sat down on the second step, pulling her stout housekeeper down with her. "Talk with me a minute," she finally managed to say. "I need to–"

"You need to rest," Louisa interrupted, cradling her arms in her arms. "You need to adjust. You've been through so much so quickly in the last week."

Joanna touched her fingertips to her warm forehead. "I feel like I've just been dropped from a whirlwind. And Father ... he–"

"Your father's a difficult man, to be sure, Joanna, and he was exceptionally harsh with both of us today. But you know he loves you and wants only the best for you."

Joanna shook her head. "Sometimes I wonder..." She shot Louisa a furtive, hurting glance.

Louisa rubbed her back with comforting softness. "Try to be patient with him, especially now. For some reason, he cared for Steven, and I believe he is grieving deeply over his death." Her dark brown eyes took on a faraway look as she added, "He really admired the man."

"That's because he didn't have to live with him. If he had, then he would have come to know Steven as a man of a thousand faces – a thousand moods." She looked at Louisa apologetically. "No one knows that better than you."

"Let's have no more of that," Louisa reprimanded gently. "It's all behind us now. Steven can never hurt you again." She pressed Joanna closer to her. "How about a nice hot bath? Then, when you come back down stairs, we'll have some tea, and you can rest by the fire."

Joanna smiled and hugged her, then rose and slowly climbed the stairs. On her ascent, she began to remove photographs of herself and Steven that hung at various intervals along the wall lining the staircase. She moved as if in a trance, not thinking about why she was removing them, only knowing she must. When she came to the top of the landing, she had gathered seven silver-framed pictures. After glancing at each of them, she walked slowly to Steven's bedroom. It was a room she had been allowed to enter only once. The sight of its pale green walls and massive carved four-poster bed brought back total recall of that single occasion.

Steven had taken to his bed with a virus, and from her room across the hall, Joanna had heard him coughing and stirring restlessly. Without bothering to cover her scantily-clad body, she had entered the room without knocking and waiting for permission. Seeing him in such distress, she had immediately telephoned her father. When he arrived, she wanted to return to her own room instead of going back to Steven's room, which he'd declared off-limits to her since their wedding night. But, in deference to their professional charade of a happily-married couple, she sat on the edge of the bed and made a valiant effort to appear comfortable in Steven's room while her father administered an antibiotic. She had never entered his room again until today.

As she looked around now, she saw the room was as immaculate as he had been. Still supporting the framed photos with one arm against her chest, she strolled to his huge walk-in closet where his fashionably elite wardrobe – including his vast array of tuxedos and suits – hung meticulously, with his shoes lined up neatly in two rows beneath. Meandering out of the closet, she noticed a long, narrow cherry chest nestled in the right-hand corner of the room. Curious, she opened it and found memorabilia from the many exciting and exotic places where Steven, and oftentimes she, had performed.

Without deliberation, she opened her arms and let the photographs fall where they may. Some of the glass shattered on the polished hardwood floor, and the rest of the frames plunged into the cedar-lined chest. She was in another world now, laughing almost hysterically instead of crying. Returning to the closet, she grabbed up all of Steven's clothes and dropped them into the open chest, bellowing, "God damn you, Yvonne Martell! And damn *you*, Steven! Are you happy now? Did you get what you wanted? Was all my suffering worth it? I hope so, because I'm done suffering for the both of you! I'm going to be happy from now on, and nobody's going to stop me – not you, not my father ... not anybody!"

Exhausted, she turned to leave. As she did, she noticed a small picture in a simple wooden frame resting on the nightstand beside Steven's bed. Stepping over the broken glass and picture frames, she snatched up the photograph. The smiling images of Yvonne Martell and her daughter stabbed her through the heart. She flung the picture into the opened chest with the rest of Steven's clothes and mementos. Her heart, now beating wildly, jolted her from her daze.

Finally in touch with all her feelings, after having completely shut herself down for the last three years, she wanted to tear the room apart and cast into that damned chest everything it could hold – every item that reminded her in any way of Steven and her last three years of loveless hell. Suffocating in this godforsaken inner sanctum, she went to each of the room's four windows. Drawing back the heavy draperies, she undid the latches and flung open the windows. The rush of damp, cold air sent excitement rippling through her. She was finally free, and this was *her* house. From now on, she would do exactly as she pleased. No one would ever dominate her again.

With a violent thrust, she slammed the door shut behind her, leaving the wind to circulate with unbridled fury throughout the empty bedroom.

* * * * *

Upon entering her own elegant suite, Joanna laughed with exhilarating excitement. Those last few moments of behaving in a totally erratic fashion felt wonderful. It was as if she had been reborn. She sucked in a rejuvenating breath, feeling more alive than she'd felt in three years.

She reached into her top dresser drawer and chose a white silk nightgown, then stepped into her private bath. After turning on the taps, she poured scented bath oil into the running water. The aroma was sensual and delicious.

Once the temperature of the water was to her satisfaction, she slipped out of her robe and sank down deep into the tub, allowing the water to soothe her tired, aching body. Soon she began to relax. Closing her eyes, she let the calming sensations overtake her. Her mind wandered freely, conjuring up the memories of her days spent on the Nantucket beach, frolicking with Nick, secure in his arms under the warm sun, vowing that nothing would ever come between them.

With her eyes still closed and her head resting on the back of the tub, she automatically reached for the soft yellow sponge and began directing the silky water first over her shoulders and then down the narrow crevice between her breasts. She shivered as the touch became not her own but Nick's, on the golden sands of Hyannis, where he had made love with her the first time. His beautiful tanned body and broad, powerful shoulders ... his soft, full lips sucking on her delicate nipples, his arms locking around her as his knees coaxed her thighs apart...

Her breath caught, and she submerged her body in the steamy bathwater as she gave in to that memory she'd saved and savored again and again over the last three years. She'd held her breath in anticipation as Nick made the connection and began wedging himself past the tightness. Then he was in, leaning over her as he pushed slow and deep. She stroked the sponge over her chest, heating with the memory of him crushing her into the beach blanket with every thrust, until they shared glorious ecstasy together.

Then he was gone.

She sighed and opened her eyes as she pushed herself upright in the cooling bathwater. He'd disappeared without warning, without explanation, and with him went laughter and love from her life. In a wild turn of events, Steven Dalton, her piano instructor at Juilliard, replaced him, pressuring her to become his wife. Before she was able to fully comprehend what was happening to her, they were married – if the platonic cohabitation agreement he'd forced on her could be called a marriage. With a grueling concert tour, there was little time for anything but travel, performance, and recuperation just long enough to continue with the same dreary schedule. On the road, it was separate beds. At home, it was separate bedrooms. Without Nick in her life, she had nothing to look forward to but throwing her whole being into her music. And on many a cold and wintry night, when the loneliness got the better of her, she would rise from her empty bed and curl up before the fire in the living room, remembering ... remembering the short time of real happiness she'd enjoyed with Nick.

On those nights, it seemed as if Louisa intuitively knew she was unable to sleep, and would come wrapped in her purple chenille robe to sit with her and listen to her reminisce about the happy times with Nick – before Steven lied to her and tricked her into their sham of a marriage. Before Steven, before Julliard, Louisa had been her nanny, running interference with her father after her mother became ill and was institutionalized. Her life would have been unbearable if it hadn't been for the stout Italian woman, and not a night passed without her giving thanks for her loyal and compassionate guardian angel.

As Joanna glided the soapy sponge mindlessly down her leg, she realized that Louisa had been with the Reed household since before her own birth. Amazingly, Louisa had dedicated her life to Joanna, first as her nanny, then as her governess, and most recently as her housekeeper – foregoing a family of her own to become the only true family Joanna could honestly acknowledge. Joanna regretted that her mother Nina had been distracted most of the time, as far back as Joanna could remember. She never seemed happy, and she always seemed to be searching for something – material possessions or thrilling new experiences – to make her feel fulfilled and satisfied. Long before she was institutionalized for mental illness, she was already gone from the household, from the Reed family, and from the role of wife and mother. Although Joanna knew her father wanted what was best for her, she was certain he was incapable of the unselfish love Louisa had bestowed upon her all her life. And so it was Louisa she thought of as both friend and family. Through the years, Louisa had proven herself to be exactly that.

Joanna's thoughts were interrupted by Louisa's knock at the door. "Your drink is ready and waiting for you down by the fire," she called out.

Feeling warm and dreamy, Joanna dried herself with a soft, fluffy towel, slipped into her nightgown, and joined Louisa as she placed another log in the living room hearth. Feeling ravenous now, Joanna ate two scones.

Louisa laughed heartily as she refilled her teacup. "Your cheeks are pink, and with that ribbon in your hair, you remind me of the sweet little girl you were only a few years ago. So innocent, so vulnerable."

Joanna was caught by surprise, then smiled demurely. "I feel as if I've been reborn."

"I'm glad to see you're feeling better."

"There's nothing like a good soak in the tub. It puts everything into perspective, allowing me to think clearly and make serious decisions."

"And what decision have you made tonight?"

Joanna sipped her tea, then set her cup in its saucer with determination. "I've decided I'm going to marry Nick Jordan."

Louisa was visibly jolted by the remark. "Joanna, be serious. You don't realize what you're saying."

Joanna sank deeper into the soft cushions, stretching her arms high above her head. "I know exactly what I'm saying. I'm going to marry Nick!"

Louisa twisted her hands together nervously in her lap. "You can't-" She bit her lip. "I-I mean ... you shouldn't even be considering such a thing so soon after-"

"So soon after Steven's death?" Joanna scowled. "You may be right about my bad sense of timing, but you know I've loved Nick all along. So, it shouldn't come as such a surprise." She drew up her legs and hugged them, resting her chin on her knees, letting herself fall into a dreamy, whimsical mood. "Haven't you ever been in love, Louisa?"

The older woman colored at the direct question, then admitted warmly, "Of course."

"You have?" Joanna widened her eyes. "When? Where? What happened?"

"In Italy – Rome – many years ago," the housekeeper said cryptically. She sighed, then shook her head abruptly. "I don't want to talk about it."

Joanna was taken aback by her abruptness, but the revelation intrigued her. "I didn't mean to pry, Louisa, it's just that–"

"Rome was a romantic city, and the young man was so very handsome, and I was starry-eyed – in love with love, just as you are."

"That's not fair," Joanna protested. "It's not fantasy on my part. I love Nick, and I know he loves me too. I saw the look in his eyes this morning. The years apart have changed nothing. If you didn't believe it to be true, then why did you visit him today?"

Louisa came over to Joanna and sat on the edge of the sofa. Taking her hand, she said, "I knew your feelings for Nick hadn't changed, but I couldn't be sure of *his* feelings, after all this time. I wondered if he would chance going to see you at the funeral this morning. And, as you now know, he went. But..."

"But what?" Joanna insisted, narrowing her eyes.

Louisa's forlorn expression indicated something was wrong. She tightened her grip on Joanna's slim fingers. "I'm afraid it's too late, Joanna. Nick is engaged to be married."

DARK CRESCENDO $\qquad$ *Lucille Naroian*

The words cut through Joanna like a knife. She pulled her hand free and turned her face away from Louisa to hide the tears that had begun to stream down her face. *Nick? Getting married? That can't be!* She jumped to her feet. "I don't believe it! This is some ghastly plan devised by you and my father to keep Nick and me apart!"

Louisa remained seated, a look of despair covering her face. "It's not a plan, my dear. I would never agree to such a devious deed. And, I assure you, your father had nothing to do with it, either. I don't know much about the young lady except that–"

"Stop it! Stop it!" Joanna pressed her hands tightly against her ears.

Louisa rose to her feet and stood directly in front of Joanna. "Young lady, it's been three years since you married Steven. Did you expect Nick to turn into a monk and wait forever for you? No one anticipated Steven's death, but it happened, and now you are free. Nevertheless, I wouldn't count on Nick coming back to you."

Feeling as though she had been struck by a bolt of lightning, Joanna ran through the living room and up the staircase, her feet barely touching the steps. When she reached her room, she slammed her door and fell onto her bed, then dissolved into a flood of tears.

CHAPTER FOUR

*W*hen there were no more tears to shed, Joanna rolled onto her back and stared blankly at the ceiling. Unanswerable questions tumbled in her head, but she kept coming back to one. If Louisa's shocking announcement were true, why did Nick bother to show up at the funeral? To torment her? Had she mistaken the fixed look in his eyes for love when, in truth, it was anger ... hatred ... revenge? *No.* She couldn't believe Nick would purposely torment her.

A dull throb began pounding in her temples. She couldn't think anymore. She padded into the bathroom and swallowed some aspirins, then took a long, hard look at her face in the mirror above the vanity. An audible groan escaped her lips. Her once sparkling blue eyes were now puffy red slits with deep, dark circles beneath them. The sight was enough to reduce her to tears once again, but she got control of herself and straightened, objectively assessing her reddened eyes in the mirror. In the last few days, she had endured enough pain and humiliation to last a lifetime, and although she had come dangerously close to an emotional meltdown, she found the courage and inner strength to vow to herself and the world that, come what may, she would not be broken.

Splashing cold water on her face, she contemplated her life up to this point. She was acutely aware there was a sweet side to life she almost but never quite managed to savor. She still had her music and, in the past, it had served to fill the void in her loveless marriage. It had sustained her then, and it would sustain her now.

With that thought uppermost in her mind, she returned to her room. Apparently Louisa had been there, for a pot of hot tea stood ready on the nightstand. Joanna removed her robe, slipped between the cool sheets, and reached for her drink. Although the beverage soothed her parched and irritated throat, it did little to relieve her throbbing headache. Exhausted, she closed her eyes, not believing sleep would come easily.

* * * * *

When she opened her eyes again, brilliant morning rays danced on the hardwood floor. A quick glance at the digital clock on the nightstand revealed it was almost noon. She had slept around the clock, a luxury she seldom afforded herself. She should have felt refreshed, but instead suffered a return of the hammering pain in her temples. Wincing at the brightness in the room, she gradually became aware of muffled voices drifting up from the living room below.

She imagined her father had returned to badger her about steering clear of Nick. But there would be no need for alarm over her rushing off to be with him – that problem was solved. Nick would soon be taking a wife, and the lady in question was not the doctor's daughter.

More hurt than angered by that reality, Joanna flung the covers back and slid from the cozy warmth of the bed. Selecting bone-colored slacks and a green cowl-neck sweater from her wardrobe, she then reached into her lingerie drawer and chose lacy beige underthings, suffering only a momentary flicker of guilt at not complying with the customary widow's black garb. After all, she was not mourning Steven, and she refused to hypocritically yield to the dictates of tradition.

After washing and dressing, she meticulously applied her makeup, then brushed her hair into a soft flip that fell to just below her shoulders. Satisfied with the results, Joanna was ready to face the new day. Just as she left her bedroom, she heard the front door close. She hastened down the stairs, only to find Louisa tidying up the living room. "Good morning, Louisa. Was that Father who just left?"

Louisa eyed her ensemble, giving her a rueful smile. "It was," she responded curtly. "He came to deliver some distressing news, but couldn't wait any longer. I offered to wake you, but he refused, insisting you needed your rest."

Joanna sank wearily onto the sofa. What could possibly be more distressing than what she had heard the night before? She poured herself a cup of coffee. Lifting the cup to her lips, she asked reluctantly, "What's happened now?"

The housekeeper continued with her dusting without looking at Joanna. "It seems one of your father's colleagues was taken ill while lecturing at a medical school in California. So, your father offered to conduct the remaining lectures. He's due at the airport in about an hour."

Joanna's eyes widened at the news. "How long will he be gone?"

"A week ... maybe longer."

The brief respite from her father could not have come at a better time and, although she was saddened by the unknown doctor's illness, Joanna could scarcely contain her excitement. For the past few days, her father had monitored her every move, and the stress and strain of it all had resulted in sleepless nights and days filled with constant bickering.

Feeling like a prisoner who had just been granted a reprieve, Joanna began mentally planning several ways to enjoy her new freedom. She was so deep in thought, she didn't notice Louisa marching over until she stood before her with a deep scowl on her face. "I know that look," the older woman said with her lingering staccato accent. "What are you up to?"

Frowning, Joanna rose, standing several inches above her. "I'm not up to anything. I've simply decided to go out today. I want to do some shopping – perhaps have my hair done."

"I wouldn't do that if I were you," Louisa admonished harshly. "I know your father is going to call you. I wouldn't be surprised if he called you from the plane. He's expecting you to be here."

Joanna's patience was wearing thin. "If I haven't returned by then, just tell him I'm sleeping. I'm sure he won't question that." Sliding her arm around Louisa's thick waist, Joanna pulled her close. "Please, my friend. I need this time for myself. You understand, don't you?"

Louisa softened. "Of course." She bit her lower lip anxiously. "It's just that ... something doesn't feel right. I-I can't explain it."

"You worry too much," Joanna said.

* * * * *

The bright afternoon sun filtered through the barren tree branches, dotting the paved driveway with patches of gold. Joanna sighed as she slid behind the wheel of her pale blue Mercedes. It was such a beautiful day, unseasonably warm and certainly a far cry from the cold, rainy, somber day before. She was so happy to be free, she began laughing out loud, not caring if anyone heard her. Not since before her marriage had she been permitted to drive into the city on a shopping spree. Steven had never allowed her that simple pleasure. According to him, there was nothing that could not be acquired through telephone or computer. Joanna was forced to make all her selections for apparel and home décor items from the numerous catalogues sent by exclusive shops and boutiques throughout the world. The only exception to this rule were Joanna's elegant gowns and Steven's tuxedos for their performances. These were fashioned by their personal couturier. But now ... now she could shop anywhere she pleased.

Feeling happier by the minute, Joanna inserted a CD into the player and turned the volume up just enough to enjoy selected pieces by French composer Maurice Ravel. She guided her car slowly down the driveway, then turned right onto Beacon Street. In the midst of heavier traffic, she stopped for a red light. Resting back against the gray leather seat, she lifted her eyes upward to marvel at the beauty of the John Hancock and the Prudential buildings; two of the many monumental structures Boston was famous for. With tinted glass windows that reflected the city below, they soared high, their colossal majesty gleaming in the cloudless sky.

When the light changed, Joanna turned onto Newbury Street and pulled into a parking garage. She fell into the hurried pace of the crowd on the busy street and surprisingly went unrecognized and unnoticed.

For the next hour or so, she leisurely toured the quaint little specialty shops, pausing the longest in the Boston Guild. The prestigious art society occupied a building of modest décor, its off-white walls adorned with spectacular paintings. One particular watercolor executed in vibrant hues of orange, green, and yellow caught Joann's attention. Without bothering to inquire about the cost, she purchased it immediately. Upon recognizing her, the gallery owner promised to have the piece delivered promptly.

As the owner escorted her to the door, a young girl of about nineteen quickly pushed her way through the crowd on the sidewalk and stepped in front of Joanna, blocking her exit. The girl obviously recognized Joanna and was taken aback with eyes wide and mouth agape. A trifle uncomfortable, Joanna waited for the girl to speak. "E-Excuse me, Mrs. Dalton," she stammered. "I-I just wanted to say how much I enjoy your music. I'm also a student at Juilliard, and I – well – I just wanted to express my sympathy."

"Thank you for your kind words," Joanna replied, trying to be polite. She wondered if the girl was thinking it strange for her to be visiting an art gallery the day after her husband's funeral. Her father's warning quickly came to mind, and she felt a twinge of guilt. Perhaps he had been right, but it was too late now. Besides, she was enjoying herself too much. After living three years under Steven's ominous shadow, she felt she deserved a little enjoyment. With a warm smile, Joanna bade the girl goodbye, leaving her standing in awe in the doorway.

As she descended the steps, her stomach began to

growl. With the exception of coffee, she'd had nothing to eat that day. She wound her way through the flowing traffic and reached the opposite side of the intersection, finding herself in front of the quaint little restaurant where she and Nick had spent long, lazy, afternoons talking and consuming pots of coffee while holding hands and gazing soulfully into each other's eyes. The memory made her sigh, and tears threatened to spill. Dabbing at the corners of her eyes, she quickly wiped them dry, then paused in the restaurant's doorway. With her reflection mirrored in the glass, she made a quick check of her appearance. The wind had played havoc with her hair, and a thorough inspection of her purse failed to produce either a comb or brush, so she made do with her fingers. Drawing a reluctant breath, she stepped inside the tiny restaurant. It was oddly quiet, and Joanna guessed it was due to the lateness of the hour. The luncheon crowd had long since departed, and it was much too early for the dinner rush.

She approached the counter and ordered a chicken salad sandwich to go, and a cup of tea to sip while she waited for her order. There were only a few patrons dining in the tiny coffee shop, each of them reading a magazine or a newspaper while enjoying afternoon repast. She sat at a nearby table and, just as she took a satisfying swallow of tea, she thought she heard someone whisper her name. Afraid she might be hallucinating, she froze in place and waited. But this was no hallucination. She turned in her chair and caught her breath. *Nick!*

He looked magnificent in a chocolate brown turtleneck sweater and tan corduroy slacks with a matching brown blazer that hugged his massive chest. He flashed a wide smile that accentuated the deep cleft in his chin, and Joanna felt weak, suddenly unable to think clearly or move her gaze from him. He stood but a breath away from her, his warm green eyes holding her prisoner while time hung suspended.

Joanna's cheeks flamed, and she became instantly flustered. "Nick! W-What a pleasant surprise! What are you doing here?"

He reached out and ever so lightly brushed her cheek with his fingertips. Surprisingly, Joanna felt his hand tremble. "Jack – the new owner here – and I are heading over to Fenway Park to get our season's tickets early. I never dreamed I'd be running into you, but it is wonderful seeing you again. Although, I'm a bit surprised to find you out alone in public. Knowing how protective your father is, I was certain he wouldn't let you out of his sight."

"Father's been called away to California," she said timidly. "I-I suppose it isn't proper for me to be out shopping so soon after–"

"Why start conforming to rules now?" he teased, laughing.

His words reminded her of a different time, when she'd been a completely different person – carefree and happy ... and loved by *him*. Dragging his hand from her cheek, he clutched her chilled hand in his. The warmth from his fingers shot through her like fire, sparking the memory of Louisa's announcement of his upcoming marriage.

Just then, the man behind the counter called out to Joanna, informing that her order was ready. Releasing her hand from Nick's, Joanna stepped up to the counter, paid for her sandwich, then headed for the door. As she neared it, her heart nearly broke. She wanted Nick to stop her, to take her into his arms and carry her away to some deserted island where they would finally be alone. He would tell her Louisa was wrong, that there would be no marriage – not to another woman, anyway. How could there be? He loved only her.

"Hey, what's your hurry?" he asked, meeting her at the door. "Can't you afford me a few minutes of your time, after all we once meant to each other? I'm sure you have lots of news to tell me. I know I have lots to tell you."

"I'm sure you do," Joanna said softly, choking back tears. "But Louisa's beat you to it. She's already informed me of your engagement. I hope you two will be very happy." Before Nick had a chance to speak, Joanna pulled open the door and ran out onto the busy sidewalk. Barely hearing him call out her name, she quickened her pace.

* * * * *

Closing the front door of her house behind her,

Joanna fell back against it. Like a marathon runner, she felt her chest heaved wildly with such force, she feared it might burst under the pressure. The short drive home in the congested city streets was a blur through the tears that flowed unchecked down her cheeks. With a trembling hand she smoothed her tousled hair, then hung her coat and purse in the closet. Feeling weak and exhausted, she made her way to the sofa. A soft flame flickered in the hearth, sending shadows dancing on the ceiling. She lay back deeper into the cushions and wrapped her arms around herself, feeling strangely disembodied, as if she were floating on a cloud, detached from the world around her. As she closed her eyes, the image of Nick's face hit her. It was a smiling face that seemed to be mocking her, and she writhed in silent agony.

Joanna heard Louisa's soft footsteps as she took a seat, obviously waiting for her to say something. "You've seen him, haven't you?" Louisa asked.

Joanna nodded her head piteously, trying unsuccessfully to choke back a sob. Louisa touched her arm to quiet her trembling. "I warned you," she said sternly. "I had a feeling something like this was going to happen." She reached into her apron and handed Joanna a tissue,

Dabbing her eyes, Joanna shook her head. "It was horrible, Louisa. I went into Les Crepes to pick up a sandwich, and Nick was there. I mean, what are the odds? Anyway, he came right to me and touched my face, smiling that ... that *wonderful* smile of his. He seemed so happy to see me. And I was so happy to see him that my heart almost jumped out of my throat. I started to leave, and he tried to stop me by wanting to make small talk. Naturally, I knew he was going to tell me about his coming marriage, but I told him I already knew. Then I got away before I became sick right there on the sidewalk."

She rose slowly from the couch and leaned against the corner of the hearth. With her back to Louisa, she let her shoulders sag under the weight of her misery, but when she turned and spoke, she made sure her voice was more controlled. "I'm sure she's a lovely woman, but I sense his affection for her is not sincere. Otherwise, he wouldn't have–"

"You're deluding yourself," Louisa said sternly. "You must face reality. He's going to marry her. He told me so himself with certainty. So, get over it right now! It's out of your hands." She sighed and softened her tone as she continued, "I can't bear to see you hurt once again, my sweet child. He loved you once, and I know you still love him, but it is not to be. You married Steven, and Nick came back into your life too late to stop that. Now he has moved on. And you must do the same."

Louisa grabbed the white paper sack from Les Crepes that sat neglected on the coffee table. "I doubt you're in the mood to eat, but you need to keep up your strength and take care of yourself properly. Why don't you at least sample this sandwich you brought back? I've got some hot soup in the kitchen to go with it." Louisa left the room before Joanna had a chance to reply. Although she didn't feel hungry, her stomach betrayed her by growling loudly. Within minutes, Louisa was back, setting a tray of nourishment down on the glass coffee table.

* * * * *

Later that evening, Joanna's father telephoned. Through gritted teeth, Joanna lied about the events of her day, reassuring him she had done nothing but rest and was now feeling much better. Her tone was apparently convincing enough for him to end the conversation on a light, happy note, wishing her a pleasant night's sleep.

After their chat, Joanna pampered herself with a shampoo and bubble bath, but the ritual did little to restore her calm. She paced restlessly about her bedroom, then stepped to the window and parted the gold satin draperies, peering out into the darkness. Pensively she stared at the flowing traffic beyond. She imagined somewhere out there, Nick was surely crushing his fiancée against him, the way he once pressed her to him – and her torment deepened. She turned away from the window and pulled at the ties on her robe in mute frustration. Feeling anxious and restless in the confines of her room, she realized she needed to busy herself.

It suddenly occurred to her that, two weeks from this very day, she was scheduled to perform at a benefit at the Chateau de Ville. Seeing that she fully intended to honor her commitment, she decided that now would be the perfect time to assemble her repertoire for the fund-raising musical to benefit Children's Hospital. It would be her first solo appearance since Steven's death, and she wondered if the select audience would receive her warmly. Thankfully, she didn't hold star billing. That distinction belonged to the handsome composer Burt Bacharach. She considered herself to be one of his greatest fans, having collected all his recordings, yet their paths had never crossed, despite the fact that he and Steven had been friends more than acquaintances for many years. He had been kind to send a note and a bouquet of flowers to Joanna on hearing of Steven's death. Soon, not only would she meet him, she'd be sharing the spotlight with him.

That realization brought a welcome feeling of happiness to her otherwise disastrous day. Holding onto that uplifting thought, she managed a faint smile as she opened the door to her room and descended the stairs leading to the basement. Converted into a soundproof studio, the room stretched the length of the house. When she switched on the lights that illuminated the white-paneled chamber, she groaned as her gaze fell upon the two baby grand pianos that stood end-to-end in the center of the room.

Moving quickly across the room, she stopped before a tall gray vault flanked by stacks of sheet music and wedged between a long rectangular desk and a steel file cabinet. Turning the vault's dial with precision, she opened it slowly and withdrew a long wooden case. She carried it to one of the pianos, intending to place the music inside on the piano bench to sort through it. However, when she opened the lid, she released a startled cry as she focused on a leaf of sheet music and the words scribbled beneath the notes.

...I'd wish to spend just one more hour alone again with you.

Haunting memories of glorious days and nights spent with Nick came flooding back with rapid speed as she stared at the duplicate copy of the song she had written for him. She moved in a trance-like state, placing the music on the piano nearby. Sitting on the padded bench, she faced the keyboard, barely able to discern the notes through the mist of tears that now rimmed her eyes. She placed her hands on the ivory keys, lowered her head, and started to play softly, but the ache in her heart was stronger than her will, and she couldn't continue.

CHAPTER FIVE

$\mathcal{D}$uring the following week, Joanna remained secluded behind the stone walls of her elegant townhouse. Absorbed with the final arrangements for her performance at the Chateau, she put aside all thoughts of her last meeting with Nick Jordan. Any notion she had had of resuming a relationship with him was now distant and unreal, so she drowned herself in music, spending long, peaceful hours at the piano.

Her father returned to Boston the day before the concert. Despite being exhausted from the flight, he came directly to her house from the airport. He seemed delighted to find her at the grand piano in the living room, engrossed in her music. Flinging his coat and briefcase on the loveseat, he smiled warmly and embraced her.

For Joanna, his arrival had come at a most inopportune time. While she was happy to see him, she was aware she couldn't postpone telling him about her scheduled appearance at Chateau de Ville. The very thought of broaching the subject made her shudder inwardly, knowing what his reaction would be. Despite his good humor, the tiredness revealed in his dark eyes pained her, and she nearly yielded to the temptation to wait until after he had rested to tell him. But, knowing her courage would fail her if she put it off, she stepped back from his embrace and slipped an arm around his, guiding him to the couch. "Come and sit with me, Father. I have something to tell you."

"Let's discuss it tomorrow," he suggested, his smile quickly dissolving into a frown. "I'm exhausted and not up to news of any sort tonight."

"I'm afraid this can't wait." She stepped nervously toward the couch.

Her father followed with a sigh of reluctance. "This is hardly the reception I was anticipating," he quipped. "Fix your poor old father a drink. I have the gnawing suspicion I'm going to need it."

Eager to please him, Joanna went to the bar and poured a generous amount of scotch into a tall glass, adding just a minimum amount of water, hoping the strength of the drink would serve as an anesthetic against the news she was about to deliver. She handed him the drink and stood back, waiting for him to imbibe. "Thank you," he mumbled.

There was an awkward moment when their eyes met, and Joanna felt her anxiety mount. She grasped for the right words to cushion the blow without setting him off, yet knew there was no way to tell him and avoid a backlash. "As you know," she began, "there is a concert tomorrow night at the Chateau de Ville to benefit Children's Hospital."

"And?" he replied, swinging a lazy glance at her as he sampled his drink.

"Well – ah, it just so happens that Steven and I were scheduled to perform at the function. The secretary at the Chateau telephoned me, assuming I would cancel – but I didn't. I am going to perform at the benefit as planned."

He started to raise the drink to his lips again, but then stopped. "You'll do no such thing!" he roared, letting the imperious Dr. Carlton Reed Joanna knew and dreaded take over their conversation and immediately turn it into another of their frequent yelling matches.

Joanna's cheeks burned, and she drew her mouth in a tight line. "You'd be wise to accept my decision and not press the issue. I have no intention of backing down, no matter how much you object."

Her father swallowed half his drink in one gulp, then slammed the glass down on the table in front of him. "You always were a difficult child. Flighty ... impulsive ... just like your–" He stopped himself before finishing the last word, which she knew would have been *mother*. "Do you not understand me when I give you an order?" He glared at her, rigid with anger.

She reared back at his arrogance. "Of course I understand, Father," she retorted, eyeing him closely. "It's you who doesn't understand. I'm tired of being treated like a three-year-old. I'm a grown woman, perfectly capable of making my own decisions *without* your direction – and I will do just that. Now, do *you* understand *me*?"

The mighty Carlton Reed pitched himself forward on the sofa, looking ready to strike at her like an angry bear. "Why does every conversation we have end up in a fight? I clearly stated before I left that you were not to engage in social affairs of any sort! And I told you why. You are newly widowed. Have some respect for the dead!"

"I have respect for the dead. I just don't have it for Steven. And I refuse to put on a façade and pretend to the world that I do. On the other hand, I would hardly call playing the piano at a hospital benefit as painting the town red."

Her father lunged up from the couch. "The fact that it's a benefit for charity is not the point!"

"Then, what is the point, Father? Are you referring to the public? The people? Are you concerned that tongues will wag if Steven Dalton's widow joins the ranks of the living so soon?"

He turned livid. "Have you so little sense of propriety and remorse for Steven's passing that you can shed your veil of grief two weeks after his death and resume your social life? Or is it that you feel no grief at all?"

Joanna clenched her fists. "So, that's what this is all about? My grief – or apparent lack thereof?"

"Absolutely," he snapped, narrowing his eyes.

Joanna tried not to look as guilty as she suddenly felt, but her flaming cheeks couldn't hide the truth from him. "I don't feel any grief. I only feel relief, as if the weight of the world has been suddenly lifted from my shoulders. If you want to hate me, then hate me, but it's true, and I won't deny it."

"Joanna, you are appalling!" he hissed. "How can you be so insensitive toward the memory of the man who had been–"

"Unfaithful to me – among other things!" she had blurted out.

Her father shot her a disbelieving glare, as if she'd just sprouted another head. "Steven would never stoop so low as to engage in a tawdry affair!"

"Tawdry affair?" Joanna shook her head, chuckling sarcastically. "Did you think I was referring to some little backstreet encounter with a love-sick fan of his? I'm talking about the romance of the century!" She waved an arm through the air dramatically. "The kind movies are made of. And it was a classic, complete with a daughter."

Her father's expression remained frozen, and he looked as if he'd been struck a blow. "Did Steven admit to this?"

"About the affair – yes. On our wedding night. But not about the child."

He muttered an expletive, then reached for his drink, quickly swallowing the remainder. "I've heard all I want to hear." Replacing the glass on the table, he grabbed his coat and briefcase from the loveseat, and headed for the door.

"*Just one minute!*" Joanna shrieked. "I haven't finished yet!"

"Oh, yes, you have," he snapped, his hand reaching for the brass knob.

In an instant, Joanna was at his side, her eyes glassy. She closed a trembling hand over his and squeezed tightly. "You're not running away from me this time, *Daddy Dearest*. You'll stay and hear the truth about your precious Steven Dalton, and the hell and humiliation he put me through for the past three years."

Her father jerked his hand free. "I don't want to hear any of it!"

"I don't give a damn what you want! You're the one who pressured me into marrying that bastard, so you're going to stand there and hear me out!"

He screwed up his face in a horrible scowl, growling through gritted teeth, "Say what you need to say, and make it fast!"

Joanna sucked in a deep, steadying breath. "When we toured the west coast, I stayed at our estate in Bel Air. Steven spent his free time with the famous mezzo soprano, Yvonne Martell, in Los Angeles. Of course you know the name, being the opera fan you are."

Her father gave her a derisive roll of his eyes, as if he still wasn't ready to believe what she was telling him. She pressed on. "Our concert schedule was highly publicized, so when he was with her, I didn't dare go out alone – I didn't want any adverse publicity. I was already ashamed of what I had to deal with privately, and didn't want the whole world in on it."

"Joanna..." her father said, shaking his head. "This is all–"

"The night Steven died, Yvonne Martell's daughter also died from complications resulting from a serious accident."

"And?" he prodded, sounding highly annoyed.

Joanna just shook her head. "Connect the dots, Father. Yvonne Martell's daughter was *Steven's* child." When her father said nothing, only scowled, Joanna added carefully, "I'm surprised you didn't know all this already. The way you kept tabs on him, I would have thought you'd have known about every bloody move Steven ever made."

The great Carlton Reed made a face, as if he'd tasted something very bitter. "When did you first hear about the child?"

"On Steven's cell phone. The Martell woman called and left the message that their daughter was gravely ill and in the hospital. She wanted him to come to Los Angeles immediately. Steven was so distraught, he caused his own death by driving recklessly in the rain and fog, trying to reach his daughter in time."

"That's preposterous!" her father exclaimed. "The news report said nothing about reckless driving. It had been attributed to the fog – nothing else."

"That's what *I* told the press. I certainly wasn't about to admit his affair to the world and make myself look like a total idiot for knowingly putting up with it."

"I need another drink," he muttered. Frowning, he dropping his belongings onto a chair nearby and headed for the bar. Joanna followed on his heels. When they reached the white leather buffet, she stared him down. "I have a right to know why Steven was so afraid of you. What strange hold did you have over him?"

"I don't know what you're talking about," he said curtly, toying with the glass he'd used earlier.

Though his voice and manner were controlled, Joanna watched a muscle twitch furiously in his cheek. The spasm convinced her he was lying, covering things up. "For now, I'll take your word for it that you knew nothing about the affair. I have no proof – nothing tangible – but I know you, and I know how persistent you can be when you want something. And you were hell-bent on having Steven marry me. Why, I'll never understand.'

"I only wanted what was best for you," her father snipped, refusing to look her in the eyes as he mixed a second drink.

She stared at him, appalled that, after three agonizing years of living with the mistake of marrying Steven Dalton, she was still allowing her father to run her life and make all her important decisions for her. What the hell was wrong with her? She shook her head in dismay. How had she let him manipulate her so easily? "You knew I loved Nick, yet you did everything within your power to keep us apart – even going so far as to ruin his chances to make a decent living."

Her father took a sip of his drink, then turned on her, glaring as he objected, "It wasn't my fault Nick Jordan was a loser, Joanna. A common laborer, for God's sake. He couldn't find a decent job if it fell in his lap."

Joanna boiled, recalling Nick's claim that her father had tried to convince him he wasn't good enough for her. When he'd mentioned losing his job suddenly and not being able to find other work, she wondered how much of his bad luck was actually her father's doing. "Don't play innocent with me," she warned. "I know you went to Nick to try and convince him to stay away from me. You also have many powerful friends in high places. It would have been very easy for you to get Nick fired and blackballed from future employment."

"Oh, Joanna, use your head! Why would I waste my time trying to ruin the life of a man who was already doing a fine job of it himself?" He took a long draw from his glass, then sighed with satisfaction, seeming pleased with himself.

Joanna stared at him, appalled by his attitude. "I can't prove it, but I *know* you maneuvered Nick out of the way so you could push me to marry Steven. With Nick gone, and Steven pressuring me to go through with our wedding, I was an easy mark to manipulate." Tears burned her eyes, almost choking her as she rasped, "I'm your *daughter*, for Heaven's sake! Yet you preyed on my youth and fear and vulnerability, telling me Steven's proposal was the best offer I'd ever get. And, at the time, I was gullible enough to believe you! Why ... why would you do that to me?"

"Why?" he growled. "Look around you, Joanna." He swung an arm through the air. "You have everything. You're a young, healthy, beautiful woman with a promising musical career. You have fame and fortune and fans who adore you ... a beautiful home, expensive car ... the opportunity to obtain whatever you desire. And you have all this because I guided you – yes, pushed you – in the right direction. I did it all for you, so that you would be able to enjoy life."

She shook her head, the tears flowing freely down her face now. "Fame and fortune and material possessions don't mean a thing without ... without someone you love to share it with."

Her father screwed up his thin face and glared steadily at her as he growled, "Romantic love is fickle, Joanna. It's the one thing in life you can't depend on. The love of a parent for his child ... that you can trust, that you can depend on. And you already have that. Let it be enough."

She paused, taken aback by his statement about romantic love. Was he referring to his failed relationship with her mother? She knew their marriage had fallen apart, but her mother had become ill. How could he be so bitter when it wasn't really her fault? And did he really expect his own daughter to go through life alone, without someone she loved to share her life? She sighed heavily. "You know I love you, Father, but I want a life of my own, and–"

"And you have it. Subject closed."

"No! No, I want you to know the hell I've been living the past three years–"

"*Must* we rehash this tired subject yet again, Joanna?" her father objected imperiously.

"Yes. *Yes!*" she hissed. "I've been *pretending* to be Steven Dalton's wife."

"Pretending?" Her father arched a brow and chuckled, then took another gulp of his drink. "You were legally married to Steven. There was no pretense."

"Well, there's where you're wrong, Father." Joanna turned away from him, suddenly filled with anger again, the moment she thought about her wedding night – the night she'd dreaded, anticipating the consummation of her vow of marriage to Steven.

As she prepared for bed in their new house in Bel Air, California, she could barely contain herself. She almost packed her bags and fled the house, regretting her decision to go through with the wedding. All she could think about was Nick, and how having sex with Steven would betray her love for him. But Nick was nowhere around, having disappeared after showing up at the hotel the night of her engagement party. She'd tried locating him, but he was just as hard to find as he had been when he'd left her the first time. Convinced that he'd abandoned her, believing she was lost to him, she'd gone through with marrying Steven,

even though she'd long since realized how mercurial he was. Worse, despite his insistence that they marry, she sensed deep down that he truly didn't love her and didn't want to marry her. And she certainly didn't love him, and never had. She'd merely mistaken her admiration for him as puppy love. Real love, she knew after sharing it with Nick, was nothing like the fear and loathing she felt for Steven. But with the wedding looming, and her father's insistence that going through with it was the best thing to do, she'd said 'I do' with a tremor in her voice, and allowed Steven to shove that damned wedding band on her finger – the ring she wore only during public engagements, then immediately returned to her jewelry case.

But, in retrospect, she realized she'd worried needlessly about her wedding night. Drawing herself up straight, she turned back to face her father, who sipped his drink, waiting for her to continue her confession. She sighed, suddenly drained. "Steven and I never consummated our wedding vows."

Her father choked on his drink, coughing fitfully for a few seconds to clear his throat. Blinking his eyes, he set his glass aside on the bar. "What?"

"After we reached the house in Bel Air late that night, he directed me to my room, already prepared, and told me to get settled in, that he'd see me later. I waited, expecting..." She shrugged, and continued. "But instead, he informed me of his ongoing affair with the Martell woman and made it clear our marriage was to be in name only!" She glared at her father, who stared at her in stunned silence. "What was it, Father? Some deal you cooked up with him? Marry my daughter and ... and *what*? What was it Steven got out of the arrangement? He certainly didn't want *me*!"

She paused for a moment and stared blindly at the floor as she tried to control the sudden rush of tears. "The humiliation..." She blinked, choking on the memory. "As soon as he let me know how things were to be, he left the house and met up with Yvonne Martell – *on my wedding night!*"

"Joanna," her father said, rushing toward her. "I had no idea! Why didn't you tell me what was going on?"

She frowned at him and turned away when he reached out to her. "The next morning, when he returned, I was packing, ready to leave him and get the marriage annulled, but he became violent and threatened my very life if I even so much as breathed a word of it to you or anybody else. At the time, I was still vulnerable enough to believe I had no other option but to do as he ordered." A tear fell onto the toe of her slipper, and she wiped her eyes with a quivering hand, her words barely audible. "He never once showed me any warmth or love. We just lived out our masquerade like two smiling strangers pretending to love each other for the sake of his adoring public. And you, apparently."

When she felt her father's hand on her shoulder, she turned to face him. "I never wished Steven any harm, even in our darkest moments. But I cannot lie and tell you that his death grieves me, and I refuse to seclude myself from the world. It's time for me to start living again, and I intend to take that first step by performing at the benefit tomorrow night. With or without your approval."

Her father stood speechless, and she sensed her confession hadn't moved him a bit. The silence that permeated the room seemed to last an eternity as Joanna held her breath, waiting for his response. He turned away from her, his shoulders drooping a bit as he admitted softly, "I had always admired Steven as a musician, and grew to love him like a son. As far as I was concerned, his credibility was beyond reproach. But he's gone now, and if what you say is true, then it is best to let his indiscretions die with him. I will neither defend nor condemn him. I only regret that I was unaware of the depth of misery you endured for my sake. You could have spared yourself a good deal of grief by coming to me, regardless of his threats. You know I would have handled the matter discreetly."

"But–"

"Say no more, Joanna. The matter is closed."

Left cold and defeated by that ultimatum, Joanna stared teary-eyed at her father. He neither blamed Steven nor apologized to her. From where she stood, it seemed that he preferred to avoid guilt rather than come clean and honestly admit he'd royally screwed up her life by forcing her to marry that vindictive and hateful bastard. Realizing that only strengthened her resolve to win her independence and keep it. Her father would never again make her act against her own judgment.

* * * * *

The next day, seated in the plush back seat of the Chateau's sleek, white limousine on the long ride to the dinner theater, Joanna gazed blankly out the window and smiled. She felt as if she'd won a major victory. She'd stood up to her father and followed her own course of action – a course to which he had vehemently objected. It was a small victory in comparison to the steady history of losses she'd suffered, but it was a victory nonetheless.

So deep was her concentration, Joanna was startled to find the chauffeur had brought the car to a halt before the main entrance to the Chateau. Just to the right of the highway, the dinner theater's wide-angle driveway was lined with glass-covered torch lights that extended up the sharp curved concrete steps. The building's massive edifice was enclosed in plate glass panels, throwing the interior of the lobby into full view.

When Joanna stepped into the building she glanced at her watch. It was five minutes to seven. The show was to begin in one hour, which left little time to change her clothes and mentally prepare herself for her performance. She hadn't eaten since lunch, yet gnawing at her insides was not hunger, but panic at having to step out alone under the glaring spotlight and prove to the audience that she was equal to the task at hand. Along with the panic, she also became consumed with doubt. Would the audience accept her without Steven? Would they look upon her with admiration as one who had put her personal tragedy aside in order to aid such a worthy cause? Or, would they condemn her for dispensing with her mourning so soon? Would they accuse her of being a glory hound? But then this was what she wanted – had fought her father so hard for. And now that she had reached the first plateau, there was no turning back.

Taking a deep breath, she headed for the stairway and came face to face with the owner, Jason Scott. Upon seeing her, the slightly built man nodded gallantly and said, "The Chateau is honored by your presence here tonight, Mrs. Dalton. Perhaps you would like to visit the Palm Court Lounge and dine with Mr. Bacharach's party. I'm sure he would be most happy to have you join him."

Joanna hadn't prepared herself for any surprises tonight. She smiled graciously at Mr. Scott and said, "Thank you, but no. This is a very emotional night for me, given the circumstances. I would like some time alone before the concert. I'm sure you understand." She pressed his hands between hers. "Perhaps you could convey my very best wishes to Mr. Bacharach, then have a waiter bring some tea to my dressing room."

"Of course, of course. I'll see to that

immediately."

Thanking him, she hurried up the blue carpeted stairway leading to the main dining area where the concert was to take place. The massive split-level room was filled to capacity with guests dining on fresh Maine lobsters and prime roast beef. The aroma wafting through her nostrils was beginning to make her stomach feel queasy, so she dashed undetected behind the stage and entered her dressing room.

She was not unfamiliar with the plush surroundings, having performed at the Chateau before at a similar concert early in her career. She smiled as she looked about the quarters. It was a magnificent room decorated in shades of white and gold, with a lighted mirror and dressing table that stretched the length of one wall. There were several original paintings scattered on the walls, and the furnishings were covered in gold velvet.

Dropping her coat and purse onto the wide sofa to the left of the dressing table, she noticed a message taped to the mirror. Louisa had been in agony the entire day with a throbbing migraine, and the message stated she regretted she would not be able to attend the benefit after all.

Joanna sighed and crushed the paper, tossing it into a nearby waste basket. She uttered an unladylike phrase to expel her disappointment, which thankfully reached no other ears but her own. Then she shook her head to dismiss all negative thoughts. She refused to allow herself to dwell on anything but the concert.

Time was of the essence now, and it wasn't as if Louisa had never seen her perform before.

While she quickly changed from her blouse and skirt into her white batiste gown, Joanna frowned, wondering if choosing such a daring dress might stir damning whispers from among the guests. As exquisite as it was, it was hardly the conservative attire of a recently widowed young woman. However, when she stood before the lighted mirror and ran her fingers over the low, square-cut bodice crusted with hundreds of diamond accents and hand-sewn seed peals, she smiled with self-approval. It was the perfect dress ... as daring and as provocative as she now felt, free from the albatross of Steven Dalton.

Joanna licked her lips in delight while she lifted the hand mirror from the dressing table and viewed the back of her hair. Instead of her usual Grecian curls, which was her signature hairstyle, her honey-colored tresses were brushed free and swirled in a thick flip just below her shoulders. There was no doubt about it. Henri, her hairdresser, had truly outdone himself.

Feeling almost regal as she twirled before the mirror, she was suddenly brought back down to earth by an enthusiastic knock at the door. A waiter entered at her beckoning and smiled when he briefly set eyes on her. He placed the tray with its china cup and saucer and silver pot of tea on the table before her, then made a quick exit as she expressed her appreciation. When she lifted the pot to pour her tea, she noticed a slip of paper that had been tucked under it. Unfolding it quickly, she sank to the velvety chair and read the message. Due to an emergency at the hospital, her father also would not be able to attend the concert. Her mind whirled with disappointment. First Louisa, and now her father. The coincidence was uncanny.

A second knock at the door jolted her upright. "Ten minutes, Mrs. Dalton."

She took a quick sip of the tea, then quickly rose from her seat and peered again at her reflection in the mirror. Expelling her breath with a long sigh, she assured herself that everything would be fine. She didn't need Louisa and her father to be present – it wasn't like she was some child depending on the moral support of her parents at a school recital. She was a trained professional, well-schooled in the knowledge that no matter what, *the show must go on!*

Closing the door behind her, she crossed the hall and stepped to the side of the stage. Adrenalin flowed rapidly throughout her body, yet she remained calm and poised as the master of ceremonies introduced her, and she stepped out into the spotlight on stage. The audience rose to their feet in thunderous applause that continued for a full minute before it subsided. All thoughts fled Joanna's mind as she gave her full attention to her music. She played as she had never played before, and when she rose from the piano some twenty minutes later, the audience went wild. Tears of joy glistened in her eyes as she scanned the vast audience. They had accepted her for who she was, and not for what she had once been – Steven Dalton's protégé. Over the roar of the applause that rang throughout the dinner theater, she stood firmly convinced that she could make it professionally without Steven.

She was bowing gracefully on her final curtain call, when a page wove his way through the elegant crowd and placed a bouquet of American Beauty roses in her arms. Tossing kisses of gratitude back to the energetic crowd, she waited for the curtain to close, then walked back to her dressing room, reading the tiny card wedged between the flowers. *Happy Independence Day!* the card said. It was signed by her father with love and admiration. It was all over. She had not only won the battle, she had won the war ... hadn't she?

* * * * *

Joanna approached the vanity table in her dressing room, curious about the second arrangement of flowers – twelve velvety pink roses. She searched around the crystal vase, looking for a card, but there was none.

"They're from me," the familiar husky voice said softly.

Joanna whirled around with a sharp intake of breath, surprised to see the tall, tuxedo-clad figure stretched out lazily on the sofa behind her. "Nick!" she cried in astonishment. "What are you doing here?"

"I'm an invited guest, like all those other fancy folks out there. Would you like to see my ticket?"

"Don't be facetious," she rebuked, unable to ignore the wild pounding of her heart.

Nick raised a dark eyebrow and regarded her impassively. "I assure you, Mrs. Dalton, my presence here tonight is quite aboveboard. Jordan Construction Company has donated a considerable sum to the Children's Hospital fund." His mouth was set in a wry twist. "You know I've always had a soft spot in my heart for children. We once planned to have a house full of them."

With a mocking twinkle in his eyes, he ran his gaze over the rounded curve of her breasts. Joanna felt her cheeks blazing and turned her back to him, mumbling, "I'm sure your fiancée will be only too happy to fill your house with children."

"I'm hoping so," he replied softly, his eyes focused on her reflection as she looked back at him in the mirror.

Joanna fingered the delicate petals of one of the roses. "My best wishes to you, then." She meant the response in sarcasm, but her tone sounded sincere, even to her.

Nick began loosening his tie, and she couldn't help but notice a few strands of dark curly hair at the base of his throat now visible as he unbuttoned the collar of his shirt. Their eyes were locked together, and the hurt she once again experienced was almost unbearable. She didn't want to be possessed by him, didn't want him to hold that power over her – yet, the truth was, he still possessed her very soul.

"Why did you come to my dressing room?" she demanded. "Haven't you hurt me enough?" Her mouth started quivering, and she looked aside so that he couldn't see her glassy eyes in the mirror. "You're a cruel, heartless bastard, Nick, and I really don't want you anywhere near me!"

A smile traced his lips as he rose and moved slowly to her side, like a panther on the prowl. "You know you don't mean that," he murmured, placing his hard fingers on her soft white shoulders. His touch sent shivers down her spine, and her throat suddenly felt dry. She wanted to move away from him, but she couldn't. For a long, languorous moment, she peered into the reflection of his warm green eyes with her cool blue ones. She could feel his heart beating hard against her. He turned her toward him and rubbed his face against hers, seeking her mouth with his. When their lips finally met, she was beyond coherent thought.

"Oh, baby, my beautiful sweetheart," he groaned huskily, spreading hot kisses across her face, continuing down to the hollow of her throat. His hands moved slowly from her shoulders down to the small of her back, pressing her so tightly to him, she felt his hardness between them.

With a supreme effort, she pushed herself away from him, her head still reeling from the kiss. "What the hell do you think you're doing?" she chastised, finally coming to her senses. "You've already got another woman in your life, and I was told you're planning to marry her. Yet, here you are, cheating on her already. Poor thing. I feel sorry for her!"

Nick gave her a deep, sexy laugh that nearly broke her resolve. "You're absolutely right, my angel. I am getting married. I'm madly in love with this woman."

Joanna snorted, suddenly mad enough to spit fire. "Then what are you doing here – with *me*?"

"The woman I intend to marry ... the woman I'm madly in love with – is *you!*"

CHAPTER SIX

$\mathcal{J}$oanna paled at Nick's audacity. She wanted him more than she dared admit to herself, but she would not allow him to trifle with her emotions. "Louisa said you told her you were engaged – to another woman!"

"Louisa misunderstood. I told her I was engaged to be married, but I was talking about *you.*"

"What right do you have, waltzing back into my life, so confident that I'll marry you?"

Nick moved forward and took her hands in his, brushing them slowly against his cheeks. A smile played on his lips as he narrowed his eyes. "Oh, you'll marry me, all right."

"Are you sure about that?" she countered, trying to glare back at him.

"Not a doubt in my mind."

Joanna stepped back, but he tightened his grip on her hands just enough to prevent her from disengaging from him. "You're a conceited, pompous ass."

"And you're beautiful when you're angry."

He was laughing at her now, which only made

her angrier. "Let me go! Now!"

"It isn't conceit, Joanna," he said easily, still maintaining a hold on her hands so she couldn't get away. "I'm merely being honest. My feelings for you haven't changed. The day we met in the restaurant, I was sure you still loved me too. We're two of a kind, and we belong together. So, stop wasting time and admit it."

Joanna finally managed to pull herself free from his grasp. Finding the sofa close by, she slumped down on it. At that moment, she was convinced she could almost bring herself to hate him. His superior attitude infuriated her so much, she was tempted to grab the crystal lamp that was just inches from her fingers and hurl it at him. But, weighing the consequences, she quickly reconsidered and released her fury by gripping the arm of the sofa until her knuckles turned white.

Shaking his head in amusement, Nick hovered over her, the same mocking smile fixed lazily on his lips. His hands, wedged deep inside his pants pockets, stretched the silk material taut over his powerful thighs. She forced herself not to admire the view. Even though she had dreamed for the last three years of being with him again, right now it was the last thing in the world she wanted to do. With his attitude, she was not about to fall willingly into his arms in the way he surely expected. She had her pride and dignity to maintain. And yet...

She looked up at him, and all her feelings

surfaced in a rush of tears. "You left me *twice*, Nick! Without so much as a word. What was I to think? You were gone, and ... and ... I married *another man*, for God's sake! I stayed married to him for three years, and, in all that time, I never heard from you. Not once!" She closed her eyes, unable to continue, hating herself for allowing her vulnerability to emerge so easily.

"I'm sorry, Joanna ... so deeply, regretfully sorry," he said tenderly, dropping down beside her and drawing her into the circle of his arms.

Her defenses crumbled at his touch, so warm and loving. The joy of the past came flooding back, but she fought it down, not ready to yield, not ready to trust him and be hurt yet again. "Oh, Nick!" She put a weak hand against his hard chest. "I ... I just can't do this. I love you, but I can't trust you. You've hurt me too much, and I can't handle more of that. I've suffered enough. Please..."

Teary-eyed, she tried to push him away, but he hugged her tighter, rubbing his cheek against hers as he whispered, "Joanna, please ... have faith in me. I promise I won't let you down this time. Before ... there were a lot of things going on that you knew nothing about. If you had known, you never would have married Steven Dalton. I tried to convince you not to marry him, but I was in no position at the time to make you believe me, to make you believe *in* me. Now ... things are different. I've had time to build a business so I can make things right for you – for us." He stroked her hair gently. "I know this is awful to say, but even if Dalton hadn't died, I was always planning to come for you. And, I was almost ready. He just beat me to the punch. Now ... now he's gone, and there's no reason we can't be together."

Unable to restrain herself any longer, Joanna responded by wrapping her arms tightly around him. He pressed her face to his and began caressing the nape of her neck, playing casually with the soft golden waves of her hair. His heady masculine scent filled her awareness, and she knew this was where she belonged.

Without uttering a sound, he lifted her chin with his fingers and turned her face to his. Swiftly his mouth came down hard on hers, hungrily forcing her moist lips apart. She responded with a passion she could no longer suppress, moaning softly as his hands moved possessively up over the beaded bodice of her gown. His fingers sought the warm flesh that heaved beneath with each breath she took. She felt him tremble against her as he moved his lips to the dimple on her cheek, then downward to the hollow of her throat, coming to rest on the sensuous swell of her breast straining against the material of her gown.

Joanna closed her eyes in ecstasy and cupped her hands tightly around the back of his neck, pushing his mouth harder against her flesh while her fingers intertwined in the thickness of his dark, wavy hair. Locked in Nick's arms, Joanna lost herself in a heaven where no one existed but the two of them.

Nick pushed her back onto the soft cushions and pressed his hard thighs against hers. Sliding his hands to the back of her gown, he easily parted the zipper. With one swift motion, he freed the tight bodice, exposing her soft, rounded breasts to his intimate touch. A soft cry escaped her lips as his hand roamed over her. She had waited a long time for this, and she could not have protested even if she had wanted to.

She fumbled awkwardly with the buttons on his shirt, freeing his massive chest from the silk garment. He pulled her to him, and her heart beat wildly as she felt the mat of coarse, thick hair against her naked breasts.

"We've had some good times and some bad times," he moaned huskily. "We've loved and fought and given up so much, but through it all, there's been no denying that we've always belonged together – and we always will." He groaned, gently kneading her breast. "So I'm asking you again, for the hundredth time, will you marry me?"

The click of the dressing room doorknob brought Joanna reeling to her senses. She looked up and cried, "Father!"

Still in his white hospital coat, Dr. Carlton Reed stood there, a dark, unsmiling menace looming in the doorway. "What the hell is going on here?" he shouted, slamming the door shut behind him.

Joanna looked down at her semi-nakedness and felt sick to her stomach. She grabbed for her bodice that hung loosely at her waist and thrust it up over her exposed flesh. But Nick didn't move a muscle. He just lay there, under the scrutinizing glare of her father.

In two quick strides, her father closed the distance between them and lunged at Nick with his hands balled into fists. "Stand up, you swine, and face me like a man!" He grabbed Nick by the arm and pulled him to his feet.

"Father, please!" Joanna fumbled to secure her gown back into position. Her father paid no attention as he hurled Nick effortlessly against the dressing room door. His face, a hard mask glazed with hatred, terrified Joanna, and she threw herself between the two men, fearing that if she didn't, her father would try to kill Nick.

Her father glanced at her and then pushed her away with such force that she fell back against the table, sending the crystal lamp crashing to the floor. Stunned, she watched him lunge at Nick again, grabbing his shirt front to pull him close as he bellowed, "What kind of a man seduces a woman two weeks after her husband's death? And in a public dinner theater, no less!"

Nick's expression was one of stone, his eyes hard and menacing. Swiftly he flung his arms upward, breaking the hold the older man had on him. "I wasn't seducing Joanna," he snarled.

"I'm not blind!" Joanna's father said, his breathing now labored and heavy. "You're an animal! And you're determined to make my daughter your prey!"

"It wasn't like that at all, Father," Joanna broke in, with her gown properly readjusted. "Nick didn't force himself on me. I went to him willingly. In fact, Nick came here tonight to ask me to marry him, and I have accepted."

For one dazed moment, her father just stood there, trying to digest that startling bit of news. Then he massaged the nape of his neck, as if it throbbed with pain. He walked over to Joanna, still surrounded by shards of glass from the shattered lamp. "Have you taken leave of your senses, child?" he asked, almost disbelieving.

The question made Joanna's cheeks warm with anger. "For the love of God, will you stop regarding me as a child? I am an adult who has earned the right to be happy. We discussed this matter last night, or have you–"

"I haven't forgotten last night," he snapped. "But I sure in hell didn't interpret your bid for freedom as a license to behave like a common trollop, especially with the likes of a Nick Jordan! This time you've scraped the bottom of the barrel, Joanna, and it shames me to discover the depths to which you will sink, all in the name of love!"

His words tore into her, but she wouldn't give him the satisfaction of letting it show. She just stood there, dry-eyed before him, and struck back at him with his own sword. "You've got that one wrong. It was *you* who scraped the bottom of the barrel when you brought Steven into my life and literally forced me to marry him. He was your little prize package, all tied up with pretty pink ribbons. Only those ribbons had strings tied to another woman and a child – *Steven's* child!" Unable to control her fury, she was practically gasping for breath as she ended, "You listen to me carefully. I married the man *you* chose. Now he's dead, which means I'm free to choose the man *I* want to marry. And I have done so. End of discussion."

Her father's face turned chalk white as he clenched his fists. His chest heaved, and his shirt was soaked with perspiration as he snarled, "Mark my words, young lady. You have made a disastrous choice that can only result in a misery that will far exceed any pain that may have been inflicted upon you by Steven." Pausing only to catch his breath, he continued. "I guarantee you, marrying Nick Jordan will bring you nothing but heartache and ruin! And since you've made it clear you won't change your mind on this, I now must make a very difficult decision." He sucked in a deep breath, then exhaled harshly. "As long as you consent to be the wife of this loathsome creature, you are no longer my daughter. You are not welcome in my home, and I shall see to it that legal steps are taken to have you disinherited from my will."

Joanna's mouth dropped open in shock as her father contemplated her with narrowed eyes. His decision to sever the ties between them because of Nick was not only vindictive, but cruel and unjustifiable. Outside of loving her, she couldn't imagine anything Nick had done to arouse such hostility and contempt in her father. And she just couldn't believe her love for Nick was reason enough to be banished from her father's life forever. She wanted to scream out how stupid he was to punish her for whom she loved, but she knew it would be pointless right now to try to convince him he was wrong. Maybe, given a fair amount of time, her father might come to accept Nick, when he saw how happy she was.

As her father reached for the doorknob, ready to leave the room, Nick clamped his hand down hard on his arm, halting his exit. "Wait just a minute, Reed!"

"Take your hand off me before I lose my self-control and knock you through this door!'

"Not before I have *my* say." Nick glared at him defiantly.

"Nothing you have to say could possibly interest me in the least."

"Really?" Nick raised an eyebrow. "Then perhaps Joanna might be interested in learning your well-kept secret."

Secret? Joanna scowled in confusion as she saw her father's face blanch. "What's Nick talking about?" she demanded.

"Don't listen to him, Joanna," her father growled. "He's inventing things just to keep you confused so he can turn you against me."

"You didn't think I'd find out about your late

wife and–"

"Don't you dare say another word, Jordan!"

"Or what? You'll try to ruin me – again?" Nick laughed bitterly and shot Joanna a sad smile. "Your daughter deserves to know the truth about why the mere sight of me enrages you, *Doctor* Reed."

"I'm warning you, Jordan. Keep your mouth *shut!*"

Nick shook his head. "Sorry. Can't do that."

"Jordan, I swear, if you say one word about–"

"I'm an unfortunate reminder of the past – a past you still can't live with. I can't change what happened, and neither can you. And while I was in no way responsible for – well, *you* know – I don't deserve to have your vengeance and anger transferred to me." Nick eyed Joanna standing motionless, dazed by their argument. "So, now you've spread your vendetta to your daughter. And for what? For the sins of her mother?"

Joanna watched as her father's broad shoulders hunched forward ever so slightly. She glanced from Nick to her father, and back to Nick again. "My mother!" she yelped. "What has my mother got to do with this?"

Instantly becoming enraged again, Joanna's father glared at Nick, then slammed a fist hard into the side of his face, sending him reeling to the right and crashing into the dressing table. Joanna shrieked and grabbed at her father to restrain him, but he lunged at Nick again, his strong surgeon's hands wrapped firmly around Nick's throat as he shouted, "You *swine*! You belong in the gutter, crawling on your belly like that godforsaken derelict father of yours!"

"Stop it! Stop it!" Joanna screamed. She clutched at her father's rigid shoulders, trying to pry him away from Nick, but he shook her off violently, causing her to stagger back.

Red-faced, Nick had his hands around her father's wrists, trying to pull him loose, but her father seemed crazed as he choked Nick harder and roared, "That bastard ruined my family and turned my life into a living hell. And now you're following right in his footsteps. I'd rather see my daughter *dead* than married to Philip Jordan's son!"

With tears of frustration streaming down her face, Joanna grabbed one of her father's arms and tried again to pull him off Nick. Gasping for air, Nick jerked his leg upward, ramming Joanna's father in the thigh and throwing him – and Joanna – off-balance. Joanna staggered backward as her father fell against the wall with a thud, then slowly slumped forward, clutching at his chest. Fearing he was having another heart attack, she rushed to his side and tried coaxing him into a chair, but he gasped and growled, "Get away from me! I don't want or need your help. I'm perfectly capable of leaving this den of iniquity on my own steam."

Joanna's nerves had reached the breaking point, and she leaned over the dressing table, fighting to hold back her sobs. When she saw both men's reflections in the mirror – the wretched sight of Nick's bruised and swollen throat, and her father slumped over in the chair, she collapsed in darkness.

* * * * *

When Joanna finally opened her eyes, the room spun around her with frightening speed. She lay very still, slowly realizing she was lying on the couch with Nick's jacket wrapped around her bare shoulders. She tried to focus on the figure bent low above her, and finally recognized it was Nick. When she lifted her head and tried to sit up, he pressed a cool palm against her forehead and eased her back down, whispering, "Relax, Joanna. It's all over now." She dropped back listlessly on the soft arm of the couch, mumbling, "What happened?"

"You fainted, but you're going to be fine."

Joanna moistened her dry lips with her tongue and blinked her eyes repeatedly until Nick's face came into full focus. "My father! Where is he? Is he ill? Is he...?"

"Your father is fine," Nick promised, tucking his jacket securely around her.

"Where is he? I want to see him. We need to talk. I-I have to know..." she choked on tears as the vision of her mother whirled around in her addled head.

There was a light tapping on the door, and Nick answered it immediately. A waiter paused in the doorway, holding a covered tray. His eyes flew open in astonishment as he looked at Nick's crumpled shirt, still opened to his waist. His face flushed with embarrassment as he said, "Excuse me, sir, I have the soup you ordered."

"Put it on the table," Nick replied, turning back to Joanna.

"Yes, sir." The waiter crossed over to the table, pausing at the remains of the shattered lamp.

"My apologies," Nick said quickly. "I accidentally knocked over the lamp. If you will send someone to remove the glass, I will take care of the matter on my way out."

The waiter nodded his head, and his gaze shifted uncomfortably from Nick to Joanna. She flushed, imagining what he was thinking. When the young man shut the door behind him, Joanna groaned. "God, I could almost read his thoughts."

"Don't worry about it," Nick said offhandedly. "The important thing now is to get some food into you. I was lucky enough to find a waiter passing in the hall as your father left."

Joanna sighed. "I couldn't eat a thing."

"Nonsense," he quipped. Pulling a chair close to the sofa, he placed the tray on it. "Once you have something in your stomach, you'll feel much better."

Joanna swung her legs to the floor and sat upright, but the motion caused her head to spin a little, and she grasped the arms of the chair for support. Nick sat down beside her softly, and she felt comforting reassurance as his weight rested against her. He bent down and placed a kiss on her bare shoulder. "You'd better eat quickly, before I give in to my baser instincts and ravish you." He laughed softly, obviously trying to distract her, but she couldn't be prodded out of her melancholy.

She shrugged away from him, her eyes burning from suppressed tears. "It isn't nourishment I need, Nick, it's answers – answers to questions that have been haunting me for years. And I won't be satisfied until I know the truth."

"And you feel I should be the one to tell you?"

"Well, I certainly can't go to my father. You heard him. He's disowned me." She nearly choked on the words. "And all because I'm going to marry Philip Jordan's son." She raised a hand to her forehead in confused frustration. "I'm sorry, but I can't accept that excuse. I know my father. I know the depths of his emotions, especially his rage, and it spewed from him like molten lava from a volcano when you mentioned my mother – and again when he mentioned your father." She paused, and suddenly it all became crystal clear. "They ... *knew* each other, didn't they?"

Nick rose abruptly from the couch and began pacing nervously before her. A frown was etched deep in his forehead, and he rubbed his hand along the back of his head, as if it ached. The question obviously troubled him as much as it did her, and his anguished expression was an answer in itself.

"I see," she said, barely above a whisper. She lowered her gaze to her gown and began to pick nervously at it, trying to muster the courage needed to pursue the issue. "They must have ... had an affair."

Nick stopped pacing and faced her. "Joanna ... this isn't something I ... I don't want to say anything against your mother. I know the hell you went through as a child, with her illness, then her being committed and passing away in the hospital when you were so young. But she's gone now, and so is my father. Maybe you should just let it be. I'm sorry I said anything in the first–"

She put up her hand and stopped him. "Just tell me. I need to know. My father wanted to kill you tonight to keep you quiet about it, so it must be something that really bothered him ... something that's been eating away at him for years. Your father and my mother had an affair. What else could it be?"

Nick shook his head slowly. "I can't ... I'm not going to be the one to spill the beans. It's your father who's been keeping things from you all this time. He's the one who's going to have to tell you the truth about everything."

Quaking with surprise at this stunning revelation, Joanna stared at him as he retrieved his jacket from the sofa and started straightening his clothes. "H-How long have you known about this?" she murmured.

He sighed heavily. "Eat some of that soup while I gather your things. Then I'll take you home."

"How long, Nick?"

Running a hand through his thick dark hair, he

shot her a wounded look. "For a while. Since my mother told me, just before she passed away."

"How *long*?" Joanna insisted.

He turned away. "She died shortly after my father ... shot himself."

Joanna sat in stunned silence, staring at Nick's back for perhaps a full minute as she ran this new information through her mind. Nick had never told her much about his parents, except to say that they had both died some time ago, leaving him to be raised by an aunt. He'd never said anything about his father committing suicide.

In her own past, some things she vaguely remembered now seemed to make new sense. Her own mother had become increasingly delusional, accusing her father of killing someone that she repeatedly referred to as *him*. *'You murdered him!'* she had screamed one night as they fought in the dining room. *'And you made it look like a suicide. And now you're trying to poison me, to set me up to look crazy so you can get rid of me!'* It was shortly after that, Joanna remembered her mother becoming listless, withdrawn, uncommunicative. Her father had enlisted the expertise of his longtime friend and colleague, Dr. Loman, and told Joanna it was the drugs used to calm her mother that changed her. And shortly after that, he'd had her mother committed. She died there, in the hospital, all alone.

Joanna's eyes flooded with tears. The past was catching up with her, threatening to choke out any hope she'd ever have of finding real happiness. Her father had assured her that her mother's mental aberrations were just that – the ravings of a deranged soul. Up until now, she'd had no reason to doubt what he'd told her. But now, new and horrible doubts plagued her. What if her mother *hadn't* been delusional? What if her ravings had been based on truth, even a small thread of truth? Maybe her father hadn't actually pulled the trigger on the gun that killed Nick's father, but he certainly was capable of making Nick's father's life a living hell, to the point that the man may have decided suicide was a welcome alternative. Hadn't Nick said her father tried to convince him he was unworthy of her? What if her father had gone even further than just talking to Nick? What if he actually had caused him to lose his job and kept him from finding another – throwing him into a despondency so severe, that he actually believed for a time that he *was* unworthy?

She shook her head in dizzying confusion. Whatever the truth was, she probably would never know. But one fact remained ... a fact she couldn't deny. Slowly she looked up at Nick. "You knew," she whispered. "The whole time you were with me, *you knew*."

* * * * *

It was well past midnight when they arrived back on Beacon Hill. Nick stopped the car at Joanna's front door, but didn't look at her or attempt to take her in his arms, as she had hoped he would. Instead, he sat back against the plush leather seat of his SUV and stared blankly out the window.

Needless to say, the brief journey from the Chateau had been a silent one. After Joanna had accused Nick of knowing about the indiscretion between their parents while he was dating her, he confessed, but was quick to assure her that fact had nothing to do with his motivation for wanting to be with her. He stuck to the claim that their initial meeting at the dorm at Julliard had been accidental, and she had no reason to doubt that. He also assured her that, by the time he realized she was Carlton Reed's daughter, he'd already fallen for her and couldn't bring himself to tell her about their families' mutual dark secret. She wanted to press him for details about it, but she could tell by his somber mood that he felt uncomfortable discussing it. Perhaps he didn't know any more details. But, either way, he wasn't going to tell her everything she wanted to know, and neither was her father.

Men! Why did they have to be so closed-mouthed about every little thing? Why couldn't they just talk about their problems and feelings to figure things out?

At least now she was closer to understanding why her father treated her so authoritatively and had pushed her to marry Steven, just to keep her from Nick. What she still didn't understand was why he focused all his anger on Nick. Nick was innocent of any wrongdoing, yet her father hated him with a passion beyond all reason. Maybe Nick was the only person left in this mixed-up mess for her father *to* hate. Both her mother and Nick's father were dead. Who else did her father have to blame for his infernal unhappiness?

Exhausted and feeling deflated after everything that had happened in the past few weeks – Steven's death, his funeral, her father disowning her and fighting with Nick, and now this awful secret unfolding about her mother's past indiscretion with Nick's father – she wondered when she'd ever be able to relax and simply enjoy life. She fought like a tigress to hold back the tears that threatened to spill, but they sprang to the surface when she focused on Nick's rugged profile handsomely outlined in the silvery moonlight. He seemed lost in thought, completely oblivious to her. She longed for reassurance that nothing had changed between them – but, right now, their future together wasn't looking so promising.

She sighed heavily and dabbed at her eyes as she turned to the passenger door. She needed time to think, and Nick needed time to adjust to the changes in their lives too. As she reached for the door handle, she felt the strength of his fingers on her arm. She turned to face him and raised her moist eyes to him. He looked down at her for what seemed an eternity, his expression unreadable. Then suddenly, almost brutally, he pulled her to him and covered her mouth with his in a hard, passionate kiss. Going limp in his arms as the ecstasy of his touch inflamed her, she pressed her body firmly against his – needing him, wanting him. He whispered her name over and over again as she slipped her hand behind his head, drawing him down to her. Their bodies molded together, and his clean masculine scent spun her emotions out of control.

But, as quickly as he had pulled her to him, he pushed her away. In a voice she barely recognized, he muttered, "Go inside, Joanna. Go, before I take you right here in this car. I want you so much, I ache, and I can't hold myself in check much longer."

"Then don't send me away," she pleaded. "Take me with you. We can be married right away. I don't give a damn what happened in the past, or what our parents did wrong. That was their life, not ours. I only know I lost you once, and I don't want to lose you again."

Nick looked down at her, and there was no mistaking the pain in his voice. "Maybe you won't feel the same, once you think it over. You need time to make up your mind, Joanna."

For an instant, that far away look was back in his eyes, and she reached out and touched his chin lightly to bring his gaze back to her. "I'm committed to you, body and soul," she said. "And nothing – no one – will ever change that. I promise you."

"Your father knows how to wear you down, Joanna. He'll see to it that you leave me again. And you _will_ leave me, because no matter how many fights you have with him, the bond between the two of you is unbreakable."

Joanna shifted backward in her seat to look deep into his eyes, and the torment haunting his face was almost her undoing. "That's not true, Nick. My father can't take me away from you. Not this time. The problem now is *you*. You insist on sending me back to him."

"I have no choice," he said defensively. "Your father knew I would. He planned it this way."

Joanna shook her head in confusion. "I don't know what you mean."

Nick gritted his teeth in frustration. An arctic look descended over his features, revealing the anger that was fast becoming his master. Sitting rigidly and wide-eyed, she waited for him to speak. "When I threatened to expose his secret tonight, your father had to stop me, so he pretended to be ill. But, all the while, his eyes never left your face. He continued his drama until you were so overwrought, you slumped to the floor in a dead faint. Then, when I lifted you to the sofa, he calmly rose from the chair, straightened his tie, and left the dressing room. Now, I ask you, what kind of a man would subject his daughter to such an ordeal? And he called *me* an animal!"

For a moment, Joanna was speechless. It was inconceivable to her that her father would go to such lengths to frighten her. And now Nick was trying to do the same by fabricating this ridiculous tale. Joanna gave Nick an exasperated look. "I'll have you know that my father's heart condition is quite genuine. He suffered a major attack the day my mother died, and he barely survived it. Although I'm sure you weren't aware of that fact."

"Yes, I knew," he said quickly. "Nevertheless, he had already planted the seed in your head and used it to prevent me from revealing the truth he had kept from you all these years. He knows you won't rest now until you know the facts. And I didn't want to take the chance of having him suffer another coronary before your very eyes, lest you despise *me* for having caused it. So, I kept quiet. But the fact remains that the relationship between your mother and my father still affects our lives, and you have every right to be told the whole story – but not by me. I have to remain silent."

By this time, Joanna's nerves felt stretched to the limit. She realized she was making no progress with Nick. As far as he was concerned, the subject had gone full circle, and it was useless to continue. There would be no peace between them until she confronted her father, and she silently wished he was waiting for her when she walked through the door. Then finally the issue would be out in the open – over and done with. Talk about wishful thinking. It would have to wait until tomorrow. But first she had to convince Nick that no matter the outcome, it would not destroy their plans. She was going to marry him – of that she had no doubt.

Playfully, she slid her arms around his neck and

gently pulled his head down to hers so that their lips met once more in a soulful kiss. The nearness of his body removed all negative thoughts from her mind as she held him tightly, enjoying his warmth.

Nick groaned with pleasure as his strong hands moved expertly over her body, making her forget everything but the two of them. With their bodies pinned tightly together, it was impossible for her to think of leaving him. Moaning softly against his parted lips she asked, "So much has happened in such a short period of time. Are you sure you really want me – really love me?"

"You know the answer to that, Joanna. You've always known. I love you more than life itself."

"Then have faith in me," she said, pushing herself gently away. "Don't anticipate the worst. Just believe that I love you, and by this time tomorrow, we'll be back in each other's arms – and all of the worry and guilt and regret will finally be over."

She pressed a light kiss upon his lips, then moved to the door. Opening it half way, she turned when Nick reached out and grabbed her hand. "I'll be counting the minutes until you call."

Giving him a wide smile, she slid from the car, closing the door gently behind her.

CHAPTER SEVEN

$\mathscr{T}$he early morning sun filtered through the draperies, touching Joanna's face to awaken her. Drowsily she stretched her arms above her head and rolled over onto her stomach, hugging the pillow beside her. Tonight she would no longer need to substitute her pillow for Nick. While preparing for bed, she had decided to go directly to his apartment after her meeting with her father, and insist they be married immediately. That should prove to Nick just how much she loved him. A thrill of excitement tingled along her spine, and she felt exhilarated, despite the fact she had slept so little. She glanced at the telephone on her nightstand and was tempted to call Nick just to hear his deep, velvety voice, then decided against it. She could wait a few more hours. And, really, she needed to set things straight with her father before she could move forward in her new life with Nick.

Flinging the covers off, she crossed the room and entered her private bath. After a quick shower, she stepped to her walk-in closet and chose a black silk blouse and silver gray slacks, dressing quickly while noting the time on her bed stand. It was still quite early. Her father would not be leaving for the hospital for a while, but she didn't want to waste a precious moment.

She left her room and tiptoed quietly down the stairs, so as not to wake Louisa. If the older woman were up and about, Joanna knew she would not be able to escape so easily. First of all, Louisa would insist she eat a proper breakfast. Then, as she bustled about in the kitchen, she would bombard her with a litany of questions concerning the outcome of the previous night. Joanna wanted to avoid that conversation.

Removing her coat and purse from the hall closet, Joanna was out the door before the clock on the mantelpiece chimed eight. It was such a beautiful morning with bright sunlight and a cloudless sky, she decided against taking her car, preferring to walk the short distance to her father's residence. The feel of the warm sun on her face invigorated her further, and she felt good about herself and Nick, and their future together.

Before long, she entered Louisburg Square, a tiny exclusive neighborhood that epitomized the best of old Boston. Containing only thirty-one houses in the prized acreage of sloping terrain, this elegant little haven with its cobblestones, red bricks, and quaint little brass doorknobs, was noted for its charm and subtle English flavor.

In the past, an impressive array of lodgers including William Dean Howells, Edwin Booth, and

DARK CRESCENDO   *Lucille Naroian*

Louisa May Alcott had all made their homes in Louisburg Square. But yesterday's literary tradition embodied by Howells and Alcott now lived on in the Square's newest resident, Dr. Thomas C. Walker, a retired neurosurgeon who had turned his passion for historical novels into a successful second career. Dr. Walker's third novel had just topped the bestseller list, and it just so happened that his home sat adjacent to Joanna's father's house.

The bearded, distinguished author had just snapped the latch on his door when Joanna spotted him. Seeing her, Dr. Walker flashed a wide grin, and Joanna blushed deeply. "Lovely morning, isn't it, Mrs. Dalton?" he said, walking past her to his car.

"Yes, it is, Dr. Walker," she replied in a singsong tone. "Yes, it is."

Joanna vaguely remembered his wishing her a good day, for she was suddenly brought back down to earth as her gaze settled on her father standing tall and proud in the doorway of his home. His unexpected presence caused her to tremble inwardly, and she swallowed hard while walking slowly toward him. When she reached the wrought-iron fence surrounding his two-story townhouse, she stopped and looked up at him, half-expecting him to close the door in her face. But he remained standing there, regarding her somewhat coldly for a moment. It was then that Joanna became aware of his small, one-sided smile. "I've been expecting you," he said, gesturing her to come forward.

"This is not a social visit," she replied dryly, entering the house.

He didn't react to her statement, but took her coat as she offered it to him, then hung it in the hall closet, after which he followed her through a set of French doors leading to his favorite room, the study. The décor of the room revealed his lifelong passion for thoroughbred horses. They appeared in etchings, engravings, and paintings on every wall. The furniture was masculine dark pine set off elegantly with soft green corded velour upholstery. And the equestrian menagerie scattered about the room seemed as content to be there as Carlton Reed himself.

When Joanna settled herself down on the sofa, her father asked if she'd had breakfast. "No," she replied, suddenly feeling very awkward in the room she had come to love almost as much as he did.

"I didn't think so," he quipped, "so I had Mrs. Cummings prepare a tray for you." He walked over to his desk, where a silver tray of coffee and pastries sat awaiting her arrival. He lifted the tray and set it on the huge pine coffee table before the sofa.

Joanna incredulously eyed the spread before her, then lifted her gaze to his face. He was smiling at her almost triumphantly while he filled her cup with steaming hot coffee. When he handed her the cup, he said casually, "It's been a long time since you've joined me for breakfast. I'm delighted." He poured himself a cup, then sat in the overstuffed armchair across from her.

Joanna sipped her coffee and tried to conceal the anxiety stirring within her, but found it extremely difficult. All the while she was preparing to come here, her thoughts had been concentrated on Nick and their future together. Not once had she given any attention to the problem that separated them, nor to the man who sat opposite her. And now, here she was with her guard down, completely unarmed for what was about to come.

How foolish! she chastised herself mentally. Obviously her father was well prepared. He had been expecting her, just as Nick had said. The image of a sitting duck in a shooting gallery suddenly came to mind. Well, she had been in a similar position before and had managed to survive. This time the outcome would be different. Instead of merely surviving, she intended to be victorious. All she needed was clear thinking and self-control, and the determination not to let her father get the better of her. Of course, that was easier said than done. He was a master at manipulating people, and his main target had always been her. But not this time...

Hesitantly, she looked across the table at her father. His dark, piercing eyes remained fixed on her. No doubt he was waiting for her to make the first move, and she knew he would wait forever if he had to. With deliberate nonchalance, she looked around the room, then asked, "Where is Mrs. Cummings? I'd like to–"

"I gave her the rest of the morning off. I wanted

us to be alone."

Joanna leaned back against the cushions and laughed softly, not really amused. "You never cease to amaze me, Father. I almost believe you're psychic."

"I assure you, I possess no special powers, Joanna," he replied as he lifted his pipe and lighter from the wooden rack on the table beside him. "There's nothing mystical connected with your being here this morning. I knew, after a good night's sleep, you'd reconsider."

Joanna pursed her lips. "If you're implying that I've left Nick, then you're sadly mistaken. We plan to be married as soon as we can make the arrangements."

It was a blunt statement of fact, not intended to shock her father, but apparently it did. His face paled, and his head went back against the wingback chair. His dark eyes stared blankly at the ceiling while his powerful voice trembled with emotion. "How can you be so blind to let this unscrupulous man come between us? Have you no respect for me or the fact that I've devoted my life to you?"

Joanna could feel the manipulative string twisting itself tightly around her conscience, and she suffered a slow boil. The nerve of him playing on her sympathy, or better yet, chastising her for being so ungrateful for *his* loyalty to her throughout the years. What about her? Hadn't she forfeited enough for him? For as far back as she could remember, she had done everything he had asked of her, including marrying the man *he* had chosen.

Angrily, she dug her nails into the palms of her hands. "You're not going to make me feel guilty for choosing Nick over you, Father. It was *your* decision to make me an outcast if I marry him. I certainly regret that things turned out so badly, but I didn't come here seeking absolution. I came to learn about the affair between my mother and Philip Jordan. I know they were involved, so don't try to deny it."

She had placed her demand straight on the line, expecting anything but the response she got. "Very well," he said, his voice barely above a whisper. "I don't deny it. In fact, I believe it is time you were told *everything*." He exhaled with a deep sigh as he placed the pipe and lighter back onto the rack, then he slowly lifted himself out of his chair. His face twisted as though the effort caused him great pain. Ordinarily, the sight of him in such distress would have made Joanna rush to his side, concerned that he might be having a spell. But she had already witnessed this little drama last night, and Nick confirmed that it was all an act. After thinking it over, she'd decided to take Nick's word for it. She wasn't about to be fooled into believing he was ill again.

He reached his desk on the opposite side of the room. From his jacket pocket he withdrew a tiny key, and with a not quite steady hand, he unlocked the center drawer. His fingers came to rest on a white slip of paper that he regarded for a moment. "Do you recall how your mother died?" he asked weakly.

Joanna was annoyed at the obvious question. "Of

course. She died of pneumonia in the sanatorium, just days after you had her committed."

"No," he said, groping his way back to where she was seated. "I ... lied ... to you. I had to ... to protect you." Each word was expelled on a long, laborious sigh. "Here. See for yourself." He stood before her, bent low at the waist, and swayed on his feet as he handed her the paper. Joanna snatched it from his shaking hand. When she unfolded it, her gaze dropped to the words typed in bold black print.

"I don't believe it!" she exclaimed, hurling the paper back at him. "It's a fraud – meaningless words on a coroner's report that you could have put there yourself. It proves nothing."

Suddenly, his ashen-white face began to turn a dull gray, and he rubbed his chest hard with the paper before putting it in his pocket. All the while, his dark hooded eyes never left her face. In the past ten minutes, he seemed to have aged twenty years, and Joanna watched him with a keen eye, silently marveling at how far he would actually go to carry out his charade.

"There's more in the desk," he mumbled, dragging himself back to his chair. When he got there, he removed a handkerchief from his pants pocket. "A ... a copy of a ... desk register ... from a hotel ... in New York." He paused to wipe the perspiration that was streaming down his face. "And ... a police report."

"That's enough!" she flared savagely, watching him sink into the chair and lower his head into his hand.

"It's what you wanted to hear," he said, barely above a whisper. "Now, if you don't mind ... we'll talk about this later. I'm not up to it right now."

"Cut the dramatics!" she snapped, jumping to her feet. "You don't fool me one bit."

"Please ... Joanna," he begged.

Joanna flatly disregarded his plea. She'd had her fill of this whole melodramatic scene. Defiantly she rounded the coffee table and stood inches away from him. "We can save ourselves a lot of time and energy if you'll stop this ridiculous sideshow and explain her death to me and how Nick ties into it. Then I'll leave so you can get all the rest you so badly need!"

It was as if Joanna had ignited a fuse under him. He gripped the arms of his chair so hard, his knuckles turned white from the pressure, then he pushed himself out of the chair. His chalk-white face turned crimson, and his lips thinned in a hard, tight line.

The sudden transformation caused Joanna to gasp as she automatically stepped back toward the sofa, but her father's hand clamped hard around her thin wrist, holding her there. All the strength he could generate was concentrated in his hand, and Joanna thought her wrist would break in two. Although she wanted to cry out in pain, she dared not, for the violence in his eyes defied her to even so much as breathe.

His breaths came in rapid spasms, and Joanna imagined the devil himself was about to spring forth as he spewed, "Philip Jordan murdered your mother!" The force of his words nearly knocked her over. "He didn't do it himself, but it was the same thing! She died trying to abort *his* baby!"

Joanna gasped.

"You want the truth? Then shut up and listen!" he roared viciously. "Your mother and I – and you – were living in Waltham at the time. We had a guesthouse on the property that needed some repairs. Philip Jordan was a carpenter who came to us highly recommended. Your mother fell hopelessly in love with him, but he only used her to get to my money. He thought by taking her away from me that I would pay any price to get her back. But he was wrong. I was well rid of her. Then, when she found out she was pregnant, the bastard figured he really had me. He threatened to go to the press and spread our good name all over the newspapers if I didn't pay him a hundred thousand dollars. I had no choice but to give it to him. I had to protect my reputation, and I had to protect *you*. When he got the money, your mother thought they would run away together, but he threw her aside like garbage.

"A month later, he was reported dead. I don't know what happened. Some kind of accident with a gun. That was when your mother became uncontrollable to the point of paranoia, accusing me of all kinds of crazy things."

"And that's when you called Dr. Loman for help, to subdue her with drugs? I remember that, you know.

How does that fit into your story, Father?"

By now, her father could scarcely breathe. His chest began to heave under his smoking jacket, and he tightened his grip on her wrist to support himself. "Yes," he rasped. "Gene lent a hand to help me deal with her. He sedated her. But after a time, she developed a resistance. One night, after everyone was asleep, she took some pills from my bag and went to New York. She tried to abort the baby herself in a sleazy little hotel room, and died as a result – all because of Jordan! He made my life a living hell, and I will hate that man and his son until the day I die!"

Joanna glared at him. "So, the story about having her committed to the hospital, where she supposedly died, was just another lie to cover up the truth?" If he had expected her attitude to change because of the horrific facts he'd presented, he was wrong. It was bad enough he had lived his life in torment and hate for Philip Jordan, but for him to inflict the punishment of a fake heart attack on her simply because she wanted to marry the man's son, was not only ruthless – it was despicable!

Blinded by her anger, she thrust her hand out with such force that he lost his balance and fell into the chair. The impact brought his hands to clutch at his chest, and he began to cough laboriously. "My pills..." he choked out. "Get ... me ... my ... pills. In the bedroom. Hurry!"

Joanna just stood there, her arms folded over her wildly beating chest, looking down at the once giant of a man who was her father. Only now, he was not so colossal, not so menacing, but rather small and pitiable with his body slumped to the side of the chair.

When his coughing finally stopped, and his hands dropped limply into his lap, Joanna lowered herself to her knees before him. She reached up to press her hand to his chest and felt his heart still beating normally. Somehow, she knew it would be.

"Look at me!" she commanded through clenched teeth, and her father slowly raised his heavy lids to meet her angry stare. Her mouth twisted in her fury as she cried, "Why are you doing this? Have you no dignity? No self-respect? Do you hate me so much that you want me to be as miserable as you?" Her bottom lip quivered uncontrollably, and hot, burning tears filled her eyes. "For what it's worth, Father, I know all too well the grief and humiliation mother's infidelity has caused you. And it's clear to me now why hatred and bitterness for Philip Jordan eats at your very soul. But you have no right to feed your grief by hating his son. I love him. And if that means you hate me too, then so be it. I'm going to marry him. Now, put *that* in your pipe and smoke it!"

Even now, as their final parting became a stark reality, her father did not react. No longer able to bear the sight of him, Joanna turned and ran from the room. As soon as she grabbed her coat from the closet, she was out the door, nearly tripping over her feet in an effort to get as far away from him as possible. But, the faster she ran, the clearer the image of her father's chalk-white face throbbed mind. When she finally swung through her front door, she fell back against it, panting with exhaustion. Rivulets of perspiration were running down her face, and her hair had freed itself of its ribbon so that it hung in disarray around her shoulders. Her mouth was dry and parched, and she moistened her lips with her tongue as she drew in long, deep breaths.

At that moment, Louisa whirled into the shadows of the foyer, and seeing Joanna in such dishevelment, put her hand to her mouth and gasped, "Good Lord, Joanna, what's happened? Are you all right?"

Immediately, Joanna's eyes glistened with tears, but instead of crying, she began to laugh almost hysterically. "I'm fine, Louisa," she said, her arms encircling the woman. "In fact, I'm wonderful! This is the happiest day of my life. Now, come upstairs with me. I've got to pack. I'm going to Nick!" With that, she turned from the woman and darted up the staircase.

By the time Louisa reached the bedroom, Joanna had already started piling clothes into a suitcase that lay open on her bed.

"Tell me what this is all about," the older woman wheezed, fanning her flushed cheeks with the hem of her apron.

Joanna paused a moment, her arms laden with lingerie, and smiled at Louisa leaning wearily against the door jam.

"It's quite simple," she replied. "Nick came to the

Chateau last night and asked me to marry him, and I accepted."

"Just like that?" Louisa asked dubiously.

"Well, there was a little more to it than that."

"What about his girlfriend?"

"*I'm* his girlfriend, soon to be his wife."

"Have you told your father yet?"

"Yes," she said, her smile quickly dissolving into a frown as the vision of his slumped figure flashed before her. "I just came from his house."

Louisa's eyes opened wide. "And he gave you his blessing?"

"Hardly." Joanna scowled. "He did everything he could to dissuade me, even to the point of faking a heart attack."

"*Faking* a heart attack? Joanna–"

"As a retired cardiac specialist, he certainly knows what drugs would create the outward effects of a heart attack without causing real damage. And, as an administrator at the hospital, he would certainly have access to those drugs." She laughed at the irony of it all. The possibility that he'd faked all his coronary problems had never occurred to her until Nick revealed that her father had put on quite a performance last night. She looked at Louisa, smiling wryly. "But I stood my ground. I was determined to win out, and I did." She straightened out the clothes in the suitcase, then snapped it shut. "You should have been there, Louisa," she said, arching her right brow. "He gave the performance of his life."

Just then, the telephone rang, halting their conversation. Louisa crossed the room to the opposite side of the bed to answer it. With her back to Joanna, she quickly finished the one-sided conversation with a breathless goodbye and hung up the phone.

For a moment Joanna thought it might be Nick, and her whole body flooded with joy. But when Louisa turned, and Joanna saw the look on her face, her smile froze on her lips. "Who was that?" she asked timidly.

Dazed, with cheeks the color of chalk, Louisa dropped to the edge of the bed. "It was Dr. Loman. He said your father's had a life-threatening coronary and suggests you return to his house immediately. Apparently, he wasn't faking." Her voice lowered to a whisper. "It doesn't look good, Joanna."

I'm sure it doesn't, Joanna thought to herself. Ordinarily, she'd be so traumatized by this sudden crisis, that the blood in her veins would turn to ice. But not this time. She was certain he was up to his old tricks again. He'd even gotten his colleague, Dr. Loman to go along with it. Little did they know, Joanna was in on it, too.

By this time, Louisa had hastened to Joanna's side and began shaking her with a heavy hand. "Joanna!" she shouted. "Just don't stand here. Go to him before it's too late!"

Louisa's tone of voice had the effect of cold water being thrown on her face, jarring her out of her musings. Joanna grabbed her coat and returned to

Louisburg Square.

* * * * *

Within minutes, she arrived at the stately home, her heart pounding with anxiety. Now it was *her* turn to give the performance of her life, and she knew she had to be convincing, or the results would be devastating for her. She regained some semblance of composure by swallowing hard, squaring her shoulders, and taking deep breaths. When she finally entered the house, she saw Mrs. Cummings, who stood ringing her hands together in the doorway of the downstairs master bedroom. The matronly woman looked at Joanna fearfully and stammered, "I-I just got here. Dr. Loman is in with your father."

Joanna embraced the woman and muttered nervously that everything would be all right, then walked passed her and entered the semi-darkened bedroom. Her father's portable oxygen tank stood next to his four-poster bed. A small plastic mask covered his mouth and nose to aid his breathing. His eyes were closed, and he looked peaceful – a little too peaceful for Joanna's liking.

Aware now of her presence, Dr. Loman turned from her father and stepped quickly to her side before she was able to reach her father's bed. The deep set of his mouth revealed more anger than concern, and Joanna had a distinct feeling it was directed at her. "How is he?" she asked, giving her voice an appropriate tremble.

"Bad, Joanna," he said curtly. "And if I hadn't gotten here when I did, he probably would be dead."

Joanna heaved a deep sigh, then placed the back of her hand against her forehead and leaned against the dresser for support. She wanted to laugh, but the doctor's stern appraisal quickly made her change her mind. "We ... we had a fight, a terrible fight, but–"

"Yes, I know. Carlton started to tell me about it, but I stopped him. He was too upset."

"Did he call you?" she asked, wondering how the doctor, who lived in Needham, happened to get there so quickly.

"No," he answered, turning away from her. Joanna thought it strange. Conversations like this usually involved eye-to-eye contact, and he seemed to be avoiding looking directly at her. She was sure he was hiding something – or just flat-out lying to her.

"He was supposed to meet me at the club. But when he didn't show, I checked with the hospital first, but he wasn't there. I called his house and his cell phone, but got no answer. I was concerned, so I came here to find out what was going on. The door was unlocked, so I just walked in. I found him slumped in his chair, barely conscious."

Joanna peered over the doctor's shoulder, then gazed at her father, who seemed to be fast asleep. "Why didn't you call for an ambulance?"

He turned and looked at her father. "He – ah – he was in no condition to be moved. And he wanted to stay here. So I've contacted a couple of trusted nurses to be with him around the clock until the crisis passes." He shot a stern look at her. "That is – *if* the crisis passes."

She stepped closer to the bed. "Can he hear us?"

"Yes."

"I have to speak to him. *Alone*. It's crucial."

Dr. Loman started to protest, but Joanna's father raised a limp hand and motioned for her to come closer. Joanna waited for the doctor to leave, then went to her father's side and sat on the edge of the bed. The old man opened his eyes, and a rush of tears streamed down his sunken cheeks. Joanna bit the tip of her tongue just hard enough to bring tears to her own eyes, then lowered her head to her father's chest. His hand rested on her hair, and she could barely hear him speak behind the oxygen mask. "Joanna, my precious daughter."

Oh, Father," she cried. "Forgive me. Please, forgive me." *It'll be a cold day in hell before I forgive you,* she thought to herself.

He slid his icy-cold fingers from her hair and touched her face. "Take off the mask," he wheezed.

Joanna lowered the plastic device down under his chin. "You shouldn't try to talk," she whispered. "You're too weak. Whatever it is, it can wait."

"No it can't. I have to tell you that I am truly sorry for all the pain I've caused you. I'm especially sorry for insisting you marry Steven."

Joanna looked him square in his eyes. "Then tell

me *why* you insisted I marry him."

His eyes glazed with a faraway look that frightened Joanna. "I will," he muttered, "but not right now. I'm not up to it today. You understand, don't you?"

"Of course," she whispered, bringing her hand to her throat. "Try to sleep. Don't dwell on–"

"I'm an old man, Joanna." He took her hands in his. "I've lived my life the best that I could. Believe me, I never meant to hurt you. I love you. You're my reason for living. It's just that Phillip Jordan took your mother, and then his son was going to take you, too. The reality of it drove me crazy. But you deserve to be happy. So go to him. He's your life now. Only, please don't hate me." He closed his eyes against the tears that rolled down his cheeks.

And the Oscar goes to ... Carlton Reed for his bullshit performance! Joanna leaned back with a heavy sigh.

Dr. Loman entered the room and placed the mask over her father's mouth. As he wiped the tears from the old man's face, he said, "I think you'd better leave now."

"Let her stay," her father mumbled behind the mask.

Brushing her own tears away, Joanna pleaded, "Yes, please, let me stay. He needs me. He's been through enough, and now I have to try to make it up to him."

She leaned over and reached for the phone on the nightstand. With visibly trembling fingers, she dialed the number to her cell phone, which was tucked inside her purse. She'd set it on vibrate-only, with no ring tone, when she'd gone to the Chateau the day before, so she knew her father and Dr. Loman wouldn't hear it ringing. Taking in a deep, unsteady breath, she cried into the receiver, "Nick, I'm at my father's house. He's had a near-fatal heart attack, and he's too sick to be moved. A doctor and nurse are here looking after him, but I'm going to stay here with him until he's out of danger." She paused, as if listening to the other side of her fake conversation. "What? I don't know how long that will be." She paused again for effect and then said, "Listen, darling, in spite of what's happened, Father's given us his blessing, but you understand, I'm sure, the wedding will have to be postponed, hopefully for just a short time." She waited in silence for another few moments, then got to her feet, saying with appropriate emotional inflection, "No! No! Please don't say goodbye. Nick! *Nick!*"

She hung up the phone and buried her face in her hands, pretending to sob softly. Spreading her fingers, she sneaked a peek at her father just in time to see him smile broadly behind the mask and nod with approval at Dr. Loman.

Working hard to hide her anger, she pretended to wipe her eyes as she stood and murmured, "I'm going to go home and pack a few things so I can stay here. Promise me you'll be all right while I'm gone, Father."

Back to his old feeble self, her father extended a shaky hand and rasped, "So sorry, Joanna. But you're better off without him."

Joanna grabbed her purse and touched a hand to his head. Leaning down, she gave him a gentle kiss on the forehead and whispered, "I'll be back soon."

By the time she reached the front door, she was close to laughing out loud. She didn't care that she'd just found out what an evil, manipulative curmudgeon her father had been all her life. The fact that she'd fallen for his tricks time and time again didn't concern her at all. And whatever reasons he'd had for forcing her into marrying Steven didn't matter any longer. The last three years of her life with that terrible man were gone, but she had all the rest to look forward to spending happily with Nick. There was just one thing she had to take care of first before she finally severed all ties with the man she'd foolishly loved and trusted – Daddy Dearest. She was going to make damned sure he got a big dose of his own medicine for a change!

CHAPTER EIGHT

*W*hen Joanna returned to her house, Louisa was waiting at the door. "Well," she rasped nervously, "how is your father? Did he go to the hospital? Will he be okay? Do the doctors think he'll need a transplant?"

Joanna laughed. "Relax, Louisa. Father's fine. Did you really believe he had a heart attack? He doesn't *get* them – he *gives* them to himself whenever it's convenient. Now, sit down. I have something important to tell you. Promise me you won't breathe a word to anyone, especially Father."

"Of course," Louisa said anxiously. "What's the big secret?"

Joanna sighed. "Father played his little game to the hilt this time. He's even gotten his friend, Dr. Loman, and a couple of nurses, to go along with him. What he doesn't know is that *I'm* on to him, and I'm going along with his charade as well. I want you to do the same. I even pretended to call Nick in front of him and I acted as if Nick had called off the wedding. It's about time the worm turned."

Both of them giggled. "He deserves it," Louisa added. "Lately, he's become a real pain in the ass. All he does is bark out orders."

Joanna rolled her eyes and nodded. She rose from the couch. "Would you mind fixing me a quick cup of tea? I'm going upstairs to put some clothes and toiletries in my overnight bag. And I want to call Nick and tell him the latest news. I have to get back to Father's house. He's expecting me to stay with him around the clock."

* * * * *

Ten minutes later, Joanna stepped into the kitchen and sat down at the table. Louisa poured the tea while Joanna rummaged through her purse for her car keys. Finding them, she returned her attention to her housekeeper. "Tomorrow morning, I'm going to complain to Father that I have a horrible toothache and that I'm going to the dentist around lunchtime. I'll swing by here and pick up the mail. Then I'm going to Nick's apartment. We'll have lunch and work out some kind of arrangement where we can see each other every day until it's safe to drop the bomb on Daddy Dearest."

She paused a moment to rub her tired eyes. "Please don't be offended, but Nick and I are going to elope. I don't want a big wedding. I had one, and one is enough. I'm sure the tabloids are going to have a field day with *this* wedding, so soon after Steven's death ... not that I care. I'm not sure where we're going to live, either. I doubt he'll want to live here – and I don't blame him. Actually, *I* don't want to stay here. This place reeks of Steven. I've never been to Nick's penthouse on Beacon Hill, but I gather from your description that it's breathtaking." She took Louisa's hands in hers and rubbed them vigorously. "Oh, I'm so excited. Finally! *Finally* I'm going to have what I want!" She took a long sip of her tea. "You will come and live with us, won't you, Louisa?"

The older woman smiled, and her cheeks turned a bright shade of red. "Now that you're going to be starting a new life," she hedged, "perhaps Nick won't want an old lady like me hanging around."

"Are you kidding?" Joanna quipped, "One taste of your spaghetti and meatballs, and you'll have him following you around like a puppy." Joanna chuckled, then said softly, "You know I love and appreciate you, Louisa. You are family. And I know Nick feels the same way. If it weren't for you, it might have taken us even longer to get back together."

Joanna sighed as tears of gladness filled Louisa's eyes. It felt so good to be able to finally relax and have a few good laughs, without worrying about Steven or her father somehow finding fault with every little thing. Unfortunately, she'd have to make this small respite last her until tomorrow afternoon.

* * * * *

Joanna was glad her father didn't question her dentist appointment that following afternoon. Just thinking about being alone with Nick for a few hours made her heart thump and her blood race. Involuntarily, her loins clenched, as if she already held him inside her. She wanted him ... wanted him desperately.

She'd been so deep in thought during the short drive to his penthouse, she didn't realize she had arrived there so quickly. When the elevator doors opened into his apartment, she immediately noticed the white carpeted floor in the entryway was spotless, and there was a fresh lemony smell in the air. *Must have just had a cleaning service here*, she thought.

The door to his suite opened quickly, catching her by surprise. "Mmmm," she purred, stepping into his open arms. "Something smells wonderful."

"Let's see," he murmured, spreading soft kisses across her warm cheek. "It's either the house, the lunch, or me."

"No contest," she whispered, glorying in the feel of his lips on hers. "It's definitely the lunch."

"Thanks a lot." Chuckling, he guided her into the apartment. "Welcome to my living room," he announced, gesturing to the area around them. "What do you think?"

She gawked at the enormous room with floor-to-ceiling windows offering a panoramic view of the city. To the right, a fire roared in a magnificent fireplace that was the focal point of the room. To the left stood a gigantic mahogany entertainment center that housed a fifty-two-inch flat-screen TV and home-theater equipment with a movie and music collection extensive enough to fill a retail store. Facing the hearth was a chocolate brown leather sectional sofa, almost half the size of the room, yet it didn't look overbearing ... it fit in perfectly. Matching rocker-recliners flanked the sofa, along with end tables and lamps, while a huge trestle-type coffee table graced the area in front of the sofa. A white shag area rug over the polished hardwood floor tied everything together in the living area and coordinated with the white carpeted foyer. The room was expansive but somehow rustically cozy and one-hundred percent masculine, pleasing Joanna to no end.

"Well?" he questioned again. "What do you think?" He took her coat and purse and tossed them over a nearby chair.

Father would have a stroke if he saw Nick do that, she thought, stifling a giggle. She looked at him doe-eyed and teased, "I can lend you my *Martha Stewart* magazines, if you'd like. She's an expert on decorating."

He turned to her and frowned. "I'm sure she is. But, if I decide to redecorate, my ideas won't come from *Martha,* they'll come from *you.*"

"I'm flattered," she quipped, and she really was. She loved to decorate and had helped her father with his house on Louisburg Square when she was single. But Steven preferred to have professional interior decorators handle things when he got tired of the décor. Too many times, Joanna and Louisa, with lumps in their throats the size of golf balls, had watched in silence as movers carted out some beautiful French Provincial chairs and end tables from the music and living rooms. It didn't matter if Joanna treasured them. When Steven gave the word it was time for them to go – they went. *But, no more*, she reminded herself, steering back to happier thoughts.

Nick placed a hand in the small of her back and led her toward the sofa. "Have a seat while I get us some wine."

"None for me, thanks," she said, making herself comfortable.

Nick did a double-take. "Are you all right?" he asked, coming to sit by her side. "Don't tell me your father's at it again!" There was a slight tremble in his voice, a sure sign that his patience and emotions were fast nearing the breaking point.

She leaned forward and drew him near. There was so much she wanted to tell him – so much she *needed* to apologize for ... but first she wanted to kiss him, feel his hot, full lips on hers ... and show him that, in the years that they had been apart, the love she felt for him had grown even stronger. She reached out to him and whispered in a low, velvety tone, "Come."

Come.

Nick froze for a second, held motionless by the promise contained in that single word. She didn't have to tell him twice. Grabbing her shoulders, he laid her back gently against the cushions and kissed her hungrily, fiercely, forcing her lips apart with his searing tongue. She kissed him back with an urgency that matched his own. Her lower limbs went weak the minute his hand quickly undid the buttons on her blouse. She wore no bra, knowing he'd be delighted with the easy access.

His lips left hers just long enough so that he could move back to shed his clothes. She smiled coyly, unfastening the button on her jeans and parting the zipper. When Nick pulled her jeans down, her lace panties went with them.

Naked legs spread wide apart, Nick stroked himself, visually teasing her. Joanna slid her hand along the cushions, coming to a stop when she made contact with the hot skin of Nick's hard thigh. He took her hand and began rubbing it over himself. Joanna caressed his erection ... anticipating...

Nick pushed her back gently. Poised between her legs, he aimed for her sensitive vee, and the first touch shot through her like a bolt of electricity. She cried out for more, digging her heels into the cushions and arching her back. He grabbed her hips and dragged her down closer. "I wanted to take things slow," he rasped, "so we could enjoy this like it was the first time, but–"

Joanna groaned. "We have plenty of time later to take it slow. Right now, I want you inside me!"

He kissed her hard and quick, then hooked his arms under her thighs and held them high as he plunged inside her, causing her to cry out in exquisite pleasure. As he rocked back and forth inside her, she didn't take long before a low cry tore from her throat as she was pushed past the point of no return. Giant waves radiated from her loins.

Nick's thrusts were hard and fast. Sweat glistened on his skin and he was shaking now, just as she had. As he reached for his own pleasure, a guttural groan rumbled in his throat. With a harsh cry, he arched back, pulsing inside her as he gripped her hips hard, leaving faint temporary impressions of his fingers. Joanna eased him back down on top of her and stroked him. Finally – *finally* – she was back with the man she loved, just the way she knew it would be.

* * * * *

Nick felt a draft cross his back like a cool breeze. They had generated such heat in a relatively short period of time, it never entered his mind to cover up with the afghan that was folded across the back of the couch.

"You must be freezing," he said, grabbing the heavy knitted coverlet.

"Actually, I'm not," Joanna said, as he tucked the afghan around her. "Between the heat and the fireplace, it's really quite warm in here."

"Good," he said, grinning wickedly "I was hoping you'd eat your lunch just the way you are – no clothes, just the afghan."

"Why, Nick Jordan, you dirty old man!"

"Get used to it. I want you naked all the time – no

inhibitions within our house. I want you to feel free with me." He stooped down, grabbed his briefs and began putting them on.

"Why are you getting dressed? Don't you want to feel free with *me*?"

He shot her another grin. "Of course. But I'm going to get our lunch from the stove, and I don't want to burn the merchandise."

Joanna giggled. "What *is* for lunch?"

"Chicken Marsala," he said. "I cooked it myself. Got the recipe on the internet from that Puke fella."

Joanna crinkled her nose. "What Puke fella?"

"You know who I mean. That chef with the funny name and accent. Wolfgang Puke."

Joanna nearly doubled over with laughter. "You mean Wolfgang *Puck*."

"Puke, Puck, what's the difference?" He stepped into the kitchen. "All I know is that it was a simple recipe, and it smells wonderful."

Five minutes later, the coffee table was set with white lace placemats and matching napkins. On ivory-colored china plates sat healthy portions of their lunch. Nick had filled Joanna's cup with steaming hot coffee he had brewed himself. His, however, was a giant-size, Styrofoam cup of Dunkin' Donuts coffee. "I make terrible coffee," he admitted outright. "If you don't like it, I have another helping of Dunkin' Donuts in the kitchen."

"I'm sure it's fine," she said, raising the cup to her lips. It was terrible, just as he said. She tried to hide her dislike with a smile, but she just couldn't fool Nick. They both laughed. "Looks like you'll be the official coffee-maker in our house," he said, planting a light kiss on the tip of her nose.

When lunch was over, Nick reached across to the end table next to him and grabbed two brandy snifters and a very expensive bottle of brandy. Cuddling up close to her he said, "Time to get down to business, my love."

For the next fifteen minutes, they sat sipping brandy and mapping out their future. They would get married sometime within the next two to three weeks, and live in the penthouse. Louisa was more than welcome. Joanna could redecorate to her heart's content. All he wanted to keep was the king size brass bed he had bought for them.

When the discussion ended, Joanna took his face in her hands. Tears filled her eyes as she said, "I love you more than life itself. You need to know this, because the next few weeks may be difficult for us."

"How so?" he asked, frowning at her.

"I'm going to go along with whatever Father wants. It's imperative he truly believes we've parted for the last time. I will call you whenever I can, to bring you up to speed. Just don't doubt me, Nick."

He placed both their brandy snifters on the coffee table, then took her in his arms. "I want to believe you, Joanna – you have no idea how much I want that. But, up until now, you've been no match for your father. The old man knows how to push your buttons and hit you in your most vulnerable spots. I know your father's going to continue testing you to the limit, until he breaks you." He sighed and stroked her shoulders. "But I'm not going to keep harping on the subject. I'm just going to trust that you can finally handle him. You know what's at stake here, and that's all I'm going to say."

He slid the afghan off her. It dropped to the floor in a heap. Smiling, he announced, "Time for desert."

* * * * *

Their second lovemaking session went slower, more leisurely, as Nick had wanted the first to be. Nevertheless, Joanna reached culmination quickly, and so did he. She hated to leave him, but her trip to the 'dentist' had taken much longer than she'd planned.

Prior to entering her father's house, she pinked her cheek by rubbing in a bit of lipstick, then shoved two sticks of gum in the side of her face to make it appear slightly swollen.

Father was sitting up in bed, watching television, when Joanna entered his room. "How are you feeling?" she asked without giving him a kiss on the cheek, her usual greeting.

"By the looks of you, better than you are," he answered dryly. "I have some pain medication in my bag next to me here on the floor. Take a couple of tablets and go and lie down. You should feel better shortly. I'll have Mrs. Cummings make you some tea."

If he was trying to trip her up, she was way ahead of him. "No, thanks. I don't want to take the chance of developing another dry socket. Remember the one I got when I had a tooth pulled about ten years ago? The pain was excruciating." Pills in hand, Joanna walked out of his room and into hers. After removing the gum sticks from her mouth and taking off her clothes, she slipped into a frilly nightgown and floor-length velour robe, then stretched out on her bed for a well-deserved nap.

* * * * *

For the next three days, Joanna's father wallowed in her attentiveness, content in feeding off her so-called guilt. He went so far as to demand she read to him in the middle of the night. Always, Joanna complied ... tired, yet uncomplaining, reading sometimes until dawn, then retiring exhausted with her eyes bloodshot from lack of sleep. When the nurse took it upon herself to reprimand Joanna's father for his lack of sensitivity toward his daughter, the old man bolted upright in his bed and angrily commanded her to either mind her own business or leave his house at once.

It was an inexcusable display of conduct to be sure, but a most promising one, for it indicated a sharp rise in his progress. He was fast becoming his belligerent old self again. At the end of the week, Dr.

Loman proclaimed him to be out of danger, and all life-support equipment was removed from his room. Joanna couldn't have been more relieved.

"I don't expect a setback," Dr. Loman told Joanna confidently. "All he needs now is rest and some pampering, and he'll be as good as new."

"I see," she said softly, feeling the need again for some tender loving care from Nick. But if Dr. Loman had been aware of her exhaustion, he never showed it. As a matter of fact, since her father's attack, Dr. Loman had treated her with cold contempt, reaffirming her suspicions that her father had disclosed to him in full detail the harrowing event that had influenced his 'heart attack.'

As the doctor opened the door to leave, he turned and bored into her with a steely glare. "I must warn you that the slightest bit of stress could result in disastrous consequences. You understand that, don't you?"

Joanna stiffened, his meaning crystal clear to her. "I'm well aware of it," she said dryly. With that, Dr. Loman smiled as he bade Joanna goodnight.

When Joanna entered her father's room, she found Mrs. Cummings propping up his pillows to his satisfaction. "Will there be anything else, sir?" the housekeeper asked, spreading the quilt smoothly over him.

"That will be all, Helen," he replied, waving her off.

Joanna bade the housekeeper goodnight, then

slumped down wearily in the chair beside her father's bed. "What is your preference tonight, Father?" she asked, taking a book from his nightstand.

"The one you're holding will do just fine." He closed his eyes and waited for her to begin. After she had read several pages, she glanced up and smiled. He was sound asleep. He looked so peaceful, so relaxed. His aristocratic face was touched with color, and the deep crevices beneath his eyes and around his mouth were almost gone. To look at him, one would be inclined to say the worst was over. But, as far as Joanna was concerned, his hell had just begun.

CHAPTER NINE

*N*ot one to play games, Joanna found that her conscience often betrayed her by allowing guilt to surface at the most inopportune times ... like this one particular morning. She leaned over her father to brush a stray lock of hair from his brow, when a tear rolled down her cheek and fell onto his brow, awakening him. He immediately opened his eyes and, noticing her distress, mumbled, "You're unhappy, and I'm to blame."

"Don't be silly, Father," she lied, wiping away the tear. "I'm just tired and–"

"I'm not blind," he said, taking her hand in his. "I can see the pain in your face. Your heart is heavy with regret over Nick leaving, and now you've come to look upon me as your burden."

Right on, mister, she said to herself as she squeezed his hand. "You're not my burden, Father. You're my joy – my life. You were almost taken away from me, but I've been given a second chance. You'll never know how grateful I am."

"Are you truly convinced that you're happier without Jordan?" he asked, his eyes dark with emotion. "Or are you deluding yourself again?"

Joanna looked down at him, agonizing over the fear that her father had seen right through her pretense and knew her feelings for Nick hadn't changed at all.

"You never were a good liar," he said, patting her hand with his. "As much as I need you and want you with me, I also want you to be happy," he said, closing his eyes. "So, go to him."

Dr. Loman's face loomed before Joanna's eyes, and the memory of his warning clamored loudly in her mind. Somehow she had to convince her father that her relationship with Nick was truly over. She pulled her hand away swiftly and stood up. Her father stared wide-eyed at her as she placed her hands on her hips and stated emphatically, "I'm staying here with you. It's what I want, and you're not going to get rid of me so easily. Now, close your eyes and go to sleep. I'm going to indulge myself with a hot shower. When I return, you'd better be in dreamland." She leaned over and placed a warm kiss on his brow, then left the room.

In the privacy of the bathroom, hidden by the noise of the shower, Joanna called Nick and reassured him that their plans were right on course.

* * * * *

The following Tuesday morning, Joanna sat with her father in the living room when Louisa burst through the front door with her eyes beaming as she waved her arms in excitement. The older woman rushed to her side and dropped down onto the sofa without acknowledging her father's presence in his own house. Sitting in his chair, he raised his eyes above the newspaper he was reading, and before he was able to utter a sound, Louisa flashed a letter from her coat pocket and exclaimed to Joanna, "This just came for you. It's from Hollywood, California. Hurry and open it! The suspense is killing me!"

Joanna laughed at the woman's exuberance as she tore open the envelope. By now, Mrs. Cummings had joined them, and all three waited with bated breath to hear the news. When Joanna finished reading, she dropped the letter onto her lap and sighed deeply.

"What's wrong?" they all asked in unison.

"Oh, nothing," Joanna replied in a teasing tone of voice. Then she gave them a wide smile as she announced, "I've been invited to attend the Academy Awards next Sunday night. It seems that Steven's score of *Denim and Lace* has won the Oscar, and the Academy wants me to accept it on his behalf."

Louisa could not contain her joy. "That's wonderful!" she exclaimed. "You're going, aren't you?"

Joanna's eyes met her father's, and she detected a sad look behind his dark-rimmed glasses. "I don't know," she said carefully, wondering how she was going to handle this unexpected curve in her plans.

She knew that attending the gala event with Nick was out of the question. And leaving her supposedly ill father would not be advisable, if she wanted everyone to believe she had only his best interest at heart. Eying him speculatively, she asked, "What do you think, Father"

He folded his newspaper and dropped it casually onto the floor beside him. Then he lifted himself effortlessly from his chair. Amazingly, he didn't sway or bend at the waist the way a semi-invalid would, but stood tall and steadfast before her. The transformation was awesome, and Joanna's face mirrored her pleasure. He had forgotten himself and had stepped out of character. He walked vigorously to her side. "Of course you should go," he said firmly. "In fact, I insist!"

"But, Father," she protested.

"There are no buts about it. You're going. And furthermore – I'm going with you! I wouldn't miss this ceremony for the world!"

Mortified that he should even consider taking a cross-country journey so soon after his heart attack, the three women objected simultaneously, "You can't! You're not strong enough! It's much too soon!"

"Nonsense!" he said sharply. "I'm perfectly capable of making the trip. I've been restored to excellent health, thanks to all of you, and the idea of leaving this house for a few days pleases me to no end. Besides, Joanna needs a change of scene. All this gloom and doom is depressing. We're going, and that's final!"

Tossing the book she was reading into the air, Joanna jumped to her feet and swung her arms tightly around her father's neck. Suddenly, the world seemed bright again. She had reached the end of the long tunnel of showy grief and pretended soul-consuming guilt. Ahead now lay the bright promise of hope, and most of all, happiness.

"Oh, Father, we'll have a wonderful time! We'll party and mingle amongst the world's most glamorous and successful people, the way we once did."

For a moment, her father seemed to freeze in her arms as his gaze took on a far-away look. He seemed to be remembering a haunting experience that had taken place somewhere in the past, but Joanna was too ecstatic to wonder about it.

* * * * *

Joanna had made all the travel arrangements, and Dr. Loman had given her father a clean bill of health. The only fly in the ointment was the realization that she would be returning to the house she had shared with Steven. She shuddered at the thought.

The house was a magnificent English Tudor set on five acres of land in the select sub-region known as Bel Air. It had been Steven's wedding present to her. It lacked no luxury, yet Joanna hated it. She had never known a moment's happiness there. The thought caused a knot to twist itself inside her stomach as she gazed out the window of the jet. Staring blankly at the puffy white clouds, she couldn't help but remember that evening she had first entered the house, on their wedding day. Steven was to have given a concert in Beverly Hills the following night. Since they were going to honeymoon in Hawaii, which entailed a trip from Boston to the West Coast anyway, Joanna had insisted they spend their wedding night in their new home. It was in that house, on what was to have been her wedding night, that she had learned of Yvonne Martell and Steven's underhanded deceit in tricking her into marrying him with no intention of being a proper husband to her.

Now she was returning to California to take part in one of Hollywood's most glamorous extravaganzas, and she should have been as high-spirited as her father. But aside from the dread of returning to the house, a disturbing feeling gnawed at her insides. She had been experiencing this feeling for the past three days, and now, as the plane was about to land, it enveloped her like a shroud.

Her father was quick to notice her anxiety, "Don't worry, honey. You'll be marvelous tomorrow night. You've prepared a tasteful and moving speech, and the audience will love you, just as I do."

The awards ceremony was the farthest thing from her mind; it was the conviction that the outcome of her trip would have a tragic, almost devastating climax that preoccupied her mind.

As they entered the airport lounge, Joanna recognized the tall, muscular black man garbed entirely in black, standing out from the crowd. He was a gentle soul named William, who'd been Steven's manservant and caretaker of the estate in Bel Air. Joanna had notified him of her coming. As colossal as he was, he wove his way through the crowd with the grace and ease of a man half his size. In a matter of seconds, he reached them and bent to embrace her warmly. "It's wonderful seeing you again, Mrs. D.," he said, and Joanna couldn't help but giggle at the shortened little nickname he had given her three years ago. Immediately, his mood changed from joyous to sad. He lowered his eyes to the red carpet beneath him. "I'm so sorry about the maestro's passing. It was such a terrible shock."

"Yes, it was," she said while exchanging an anxious look with her father. Then, trying to adopt a cheerful tone she said, "William, I'd like you to meet my father, Dr. Carlton Reed. I explained in the letter that he would be accompanying me."

"Pleased to meet you, sir," William said, extending a large hand to her father, who shook it vigorously.

As they made their way to the main doors, William remarked to Joanna, "As you can see, I located your father's suitcase, but there doesn't seem to be any for you. I'm going back to see what the problem is."

"That's not necessary, William," Joanna said. "I

didn't bring anything but my carryon bag. Everything I need is at the house."

William stopped dead in his tracks, and his face contorted in puzzlement. "Didn't you receive my message?"

Joanna stared back. "What message?"

By now, Joanna's father was becoming visibly annoyed. He grabbed Joanna by the arm and said curtly, "Let's get on with it. We can continue this conversation in the car."

Obligingly, William escorted them both into the back seat of a white Rolls Royce. He then seated himself behind the wheel and turned the car into the heavy stream of traffic. As soon as they came to a stop light, Joanna leaned forward and placed her hand on William's shoulder. "What message are you talking about, William?"

The traffic light turned green, and William accelerated the car. Unable to look back at her, he met her confused reflection in the rearview mirror. "The message I left at the maestro's office in Boston," he explained, managing a faint smile. "There was ... some confusion ... and I couldn't find your home telephone number, so I called the maestro's office, the only number I had. I was certain you would receive the message in time."

Joanna shrugged her shoulders. "I had the secretary that handles – handled – our bookings call you to arrange everything. After she finished taking care of outstanding issues at the office, I gave her an extended vacation. I didn't expect to need her services again for a while. She probably left the office before you called back. I've been staying at my father's home for the past three weeks and didn't check for messages."

"That explains why you never responded," he said casually.

Joanna began to experience that gnawing sensation in her stomach again. Exasperated, she said, "For Heaven's sake, William, tell me why you needed to contact me. Is there a problem?"

William was silent for a moment, then said in an embarrassed tone, "I'm afraid so, Mrs. D. Your personal belongings are no longer at the house. They've been put in storage."

Joanna gasped. "In storage! Why?"

William shrugged his shoulders. "Can't rightly say, ma'am. I don't ask questions. I just follow orders."

A painful expression could be seen on William's face as Joanna glared at him in the mirror, and before either one could speak, Joanna's father ordered the manservant to pull over to the side of the road. When William stopped the car, he leaned forward and placed a firm grip on the man's shoulder. His voice was low and controlled, yet Joanna could see by his paled face that he was as furious as she was. "I've had enough of this gibberish," he said. "Now tell us what this is all about before I lose my patience altogether."

William looked discomforted by her father and shook his head. "I know none of the details, sir," he said regretfully. "In fact, all I do know is that when the maestro died, I was instructed to put all of your daughter's belongings in storage, to make way for the new occupant."

Joanna looked at him in horror. "New occupant! Who's living there now? Who authorized all this, William?"

"Your husband's lawyer arranged everything, ma'am," he said bleakly. "When I got your phone message about staying at the house, I tried to call you back to say I had made reservations at the Hilton for you and your father. That's why I was surprised to see you had no luggage. I thought you knew."

Cold, angry shock seized Joanna, and she slumped back against the seat as she hissed venomously, "Steven's lawyer hands my house over to a complete stranger, and I'm to be carted off to a hotel like a common tourist?" She shot up in her seat. "Well, *I'm not going!* Take me to my house, William!"

"But Mrs. D.!" William protested. "I-I can't do that!"

"You can, and you will!" Joanna ordered.

William turned his head and looked hesitatingly at Joanna's father, as if he expected him to agree with him, but her father merely glared and ordered, "You heard my daughter! Drive!"

With a deep sigh, William turned the car away from the curb and re-entered the stream of traffic. In the back seat, Joanna's father huddled close to her and tried diligently to calm her down. "Relax," he said, a smile flittering nervously across his mouth. "I'm sure there's a reasonable explanation for all of this."

Joanna pouted. "Can you think of one?"

He pondered her question. "Perhaps Steven had instructed his attorney to lease the house in his absence. After all, it's foolish to leave the estate vacant for a long stretch of time. Besides, it's safer – you know, with vandalism running rampant."

Joanna considered this for a moment, then relaxed against his arm. "You may be right. Nevertheless, as soon as we get there, I want you to contact our attorneys back in Boston. They'll settle this mess."

He pressed his lips together. "If the present occupants do have a lease, they might refuse us admittance. And if so, we could look like a couple of fools with egg on our faces."

Joanna couldn't deny the possibility of that happening. Nevertheless, she wasn't about to retreat without trying to get to the bottom of this. "We'll just have to take our chances, won't we?"

He was quick to understand her meaning, and suddenly his somber expression changed to one of mischievous anticipation, and he laughed. "I pity the poor people. They won't stand a chance once hurricane Joanna sweeps down on them."

"I promise to be as gentle as a lamb," she said lightly to reassure him. "After all, I'm involving you in what could be a very unpleasant undertaking, and I don't want you to become irritated to the point of injuring your health. That would only compound the problem."

"Rest assured, I have never felt better in my life," he replied confidently.

All the while, William had been driving in silence, but constantly shifted in his seat, and several times he rubbed hard at the back of his neck. His extreme nervousness did not go unnoticed by Joanna. *Why is he so jittery?* she asked herself. Was he placing his job in jeopardy by bringing her to the house? Had he, in fact, been given strict orders *not* to do so? Her curiosity piqued, she leaned forward and whispered, "Who's staying there now, William?"

William deliberately avoided answering her question. She suspected it was not because he didn't want to tell her, but because he had been instructed not to. When he remained silent, she tapped him on the shoulder to get his attention. He answered in a singsong manner, "You'll see, Mrs. D., you'll see."

Joanna tried not to become annoyed with him, seeing that they were so close to their destination. In a few minutes, her curiosity would be satisfied, so there was no point in pressuring William further. With a sigh, she sat back and scanned the picturesque beauty that surrounded her.

She considered Bel Air breathtakingly beautiful, with its swaying palm trees, manicured lawns, and perfectly groomed hedges sufficiently tall to obscure the vision of starry-eyed sightseers or anyone else who ventured into this man-made paradise. It was the city of the elite, the 'beautiful people' who had made their legendary mark in the show-business industry. However, it was also the domain of the current crop of rising young stars and long-haired rock singers, whose single attempts at fame had magically materialized. But fame, like any measure of success, whether long-enduring or jet-propelled, was not free. It carried a staggering price tag with it, and oftentimes Joanna had wondered how many of Bel Air's inhabitants had sold their souls to the devil just to live here.

Minutes later, as the three approached the house, William asked somewhat nervously, "Are you sure you want to go inside?"

Before Joanna could respond, the cherry door swung open, revealing Mrs. Blaine, the middle-aged woman who served as her personal maid when she and Steven were in residence here. "Mrs. Dalton!" the woman exclaimed, seeming more astounded than pleased to see her.

William left Joanna's side and stepped into the doorway, forcing the maid to step back behind the door. "I didn't want to bring them here," he said, loudly enough for Joanna and her father to hear, "but she insisted – they both insisted."

"Well, then ... show them into the music room," Mrs. Blaine said in a somewhat lower tone of voice, "and I'll tell Madame they're here."

To say the least, Joanna felt very much the intruder, despite the fact that she was in the company of the two people who had once meant a great deal to her. Anxiously, she peered at her father. He appeared to be feeling even more uncomfortable at having received a less than cordial welcome. Grabbing her hand, he held it tightly as they braced themselves for whatever was to come.

Turning now to face them, William nodded slightly, and Joanna and her father entered the house. Without waiting to be escorted, Joanna led her father straight to the music room, to the left of the foyer and directly across from the formal dining room. Tastefully adorned in colors of champagne and baby blue, the spacious room was bathed in sunlight. A gentle breeze drifted from the open French doors, toying with a leaf of sheet music that rested on top of the pearl white grand piano.

The sight of the room stirred up both pleasant and unpleasant memories within Joanna, and half-consciously she began to roam about, touching the furnishings with trembling fingers, amazed to find the room completely redecorated. Everything of hers had been removed, including her wedding portrait that had once hung above the marble fireplace. With a shudder, Joanna gazed stonily at the wide empty space. Apparently, the painting had joined company with the rest of her belongings.

"The painting and furnishings are safe, I assure you, Mrs. Dalton," Mrs. Blaine declared, walking up behind her.

Joanna flushed, realizing the maid had anticipated her thoughts. "Why has the house been refurnished, Felicia?" Joanna asked, her voice slightly touched with anger as she turned and took a seat beside her father on the velvet sofa. Then, sweeping her gaze upward, Joanna detected a sadness in Felicia's vivid blue eyes as she spoke. "Madame has been under a great deal of stress since – since the tragedy. Mr. Woods, Mr. Dalton's attorney, thought it best she remove everything that saddened her."

By now, Joanna was beginning to seethe inside, and although she hated to admit it, the reason was due to the maid's obvious compassion and fondness for her newly-acquired mistress, and her cool indifference to her. It was a cut to the quick, and Joanna had to fight hard to suppress a rush of tears that stung her eyes.

Suddenly, none of what was happening made any sense to her, and her mind whirled with a bounty of questions. If her house was simply leased, why should the furnishings distress the new tenant? Apparently, this *Madame* had suffered a loss, as she had. But what right did Steven's attorney have to permit the woman to make a clean sweep of *her* house? And who was this mysterious woman who held such power over everyone?

Oblivious to Joanna's emotional upheaval, Felicia walked over to the liquor cabinet and offered them both a drink.

"Nothing for me, thank you," Joanna choked out. Her father, however, agreed to a small brandy. As the maid handed the drink to him, she said politely, "I'll see what's keeping Madame."

"That won't be necessary, Felicia," said a soft, sensuous voice from outside the room. When Joanna turned in the speaker's direction, her mouth opened wide in horror as Yvonne Martell step gracefully into the room.

Too stunned to move or even utter a sound, Joanna watched with dazed eyes as the tall, elegant woman ordered Felicia to bring a tray of tea for herself and her guest. "You will stay for tea, won't you, Mrs. Dalton?" Yvonne asked while seating her slender frame on the blue velvet loveseat beside her.

A mixture of humiliation and resentment overtook Joanna, and instinctively she wanted to run from the house, but she couldn't move a muscle. She felt as if some giant unseen hand was pinning her securely to the couch, but the hand imprisoning her was very real. It belonged to her father. She turned to look at him and realized his iron grip on her upper arm acted as a vice against his own desire to leave. His face was chalk white, and his wide glazed eyes, transfixed on the woman, mirrored Joanna's own horrified disbelief of her presence. It seemed odd to Joanna that Yvonne Martell should arouse such a passionate response from her father. True, he was aware of the past relationship Yvonne had had with Steven, which could account for part of his obvious inner fury, but his whole body shook now with anger that couldn't be ignored, and Joanna visibly cringed when he jetted to his feet and shouted, "What the hell are you doing in my daughter's house!"

Yvonne Martell appeared almost regal, garbed in a white satin dressing gown, with her dark hair twisted in a braided chignon. She looked slowly up at him with her large violet eyes wild and fiery, yet she maintained perfect composure as she declared, "This is not your daughter's house, Carlton. It is *mine!*"

Joanna's father was so incensed, he quickly charged past Joanna and halted inches away from the woman. "*Your* house? Not by my understanding. We made a deal, remember?"

Joanna couldn't believe her ears. "A deal?" she echoed, looking at both of them. "What are you talking about?"

"Oh, God," he exclaimed, and his agonized tone was testament enough for Joanna to know he immediately regretted having made that self-incriminating outburst. Realizing he had fallen prey to his own trap, his eyes shot daggers at Yvonne, and he roared, "You will pay for this – and pay dearly!"

"No, Carlton," Yvonne said, her voice cool and controlled. "The redeeming hand of fate has allowed you to crucify yourself, and now it is *you* who must pay for the years of pain and misery you've brought, not only to me and Steven, but to your daughter as well. Frankly, I couldn't be happier."

Joanna pressed a trembling hand to her throat. "Will somebody please tell me what is going on here?"

Turning to face Joanna, her father regarded her with that disturbing intensity he always adopted when caught in the tangle of his own web. He extended a strong, steady hand in her direction and snapped, "Come, Joanna. William was right. We never should have come here. This woman is obviously insane."

Joanna shot to her feet, determined to get to the bottom of this. "I'm not going anywhere until I get a full explanation of what's been going on behind my back." She turned and stared coldly at Yvonne.

Just then, Felicia wheeled in a glass teacart. Seeing the angry expressions on everyone's faces, she abandoned the cart by her mistress and fled the room without waiting to be dismissed.

In this brief respite, Joanna's father tried to take advantage of the situation by feigning the onset of a spell, deliberately swaying unsteadily. "I'm not feeling well," he said hoarsely. With an outstretched hand, he gripped the arm of the loveseat on which Yvonne Martell was sitting. "I would appreciate it if you would instruct your manservant to bring the car around. I'd like to be taken to the hotel."

With a slight turn of her head, Yvonne gazed up at him. "Yes, I'm sure you are quite desperate to leave. Unfortunately, William is indisposed. I'm afraid you will have to rest on the sofa."

He regarded her dourly. "Then perhaps I can telephone for a taxi."

Joanna watched, fascinated, as the tall, elegant woman rose to her feet with cool sophistication and focused her eyes on Joanna's father. Quietly she waited in anxious anticipation, certain the tension that filled the air was about to explode. Her father had to know the bomb was about to drop when he pleaded with a devastated look, "Don't do this, Yvonne. Please. I'll give you anything you want. I – I'll pay you–"

"You miserable, conniving old fool," Yvonne snarled. "You think your money can buy anything or anyone. Well, you're wrong!"

Joanna's father flinched under the biting remark, and his attitude quickly changed from meek to condescending. "Everyone can be bought, if the price is right. You, of all people, should know that."

Yvonne flashed a sinister grin. "You're referring to Steven? Yes, of course you are."

"No!" Joanna exclaimed vehemently. Her father spun around to face her. A tormented gaze covered his face, but Joanna could feel no pity, only blind fury. "She's lying, Father!" she cried, throwing him a wary look. "Tell me she's lying!"

"I wouldn't lie about such a thing," Yvonne remarked, her tone almost sympathetic. Casting a distasteful look in Joanna's father's direction, she approached Joanna and took hold of her trembling hands. "It really does pain me to tell you that your father paid Steven to marry you. I wish there were an easier way for you to learn the truth, but–"

"Please," Joanna rasped, pulling her hands away and shaking her head as tears filled her eyes. "No more."

"I know the humiliation and anguish you're

feeling," Yvonne said compassionately, "but the fact remains, your father wanted to maintain complete control of your life, and he accomplished that by blackmail."

"Don't listen to her!" Joanna's father yelled. "She'd say anything – *anything* – to pit you against me. She's just bitter and jealous because Steven married *you*. She wanted him for herself, but she already had a husband!"

With tears streaming down her face, Joanna looked at her father, too numb to speak. His face burned crimson with guilt as he stood frozen in place. She hoped he was aware of the repulsion she was feeling for him at that moment, and she was fairly sure he was. Her hatred for him bubbled over, saturating every fiber of her being. Yet, she couldn't help but be angry at herself for allowing him to maneuver her into marrying Steven, just so he could keep her and Nick apart. To have gone to such deplorable measures by using blackmail and deceit to insure it, well ... Joanna suddenly felt like a prize fool. Trying desperately to control the anger in her voice, she looked at Yvonne Martell and asked, "How do you know all this?"

Yvonne hesitated a moment in retrospect, then the words came tumbling out. "When Steven met you at Juilliard, his career was in jeopardy. Performance engagements were few and far between, and he'd suffered a succession of bad financial investments. To keep himself afloat, Steven agreed to teach the advanced students at the Institute. Early on, you had expressed enthusiasm to your father about Steven's mastery of the keyboard. When Carlton went to Steven and explained about your involvement with a man he disapproved of, he offered to pay him half a million dollars if he would solve the *problem* by taking you on tour with him, and then agreeing to marry you. Even though the money was a tempting salvation, Steven refused. But, your father wouldn't give up. He offered a full million, and when Steven again refused, he had him investigated. That's when he learned about our relationship – and our illegitimate daughter."

Yvonne stopped a moment to wipe away a tear that had rolled freely down her cheek, then continued on with great difficulty. "Equipped with all the ammunition he needed, your father confronted Steven again and threatened to expose us to public humiliation. Compelled to shield me and our daughter from ruin, Steven finally agreed to your father's scheme. Amazingly, adding you to his performances created a sensation that boosted his career in a way he would have never expected."

Her head bowed low, Joanna digested the news in silence for a long moment, remembering how her tour schedule with Steven had become more and more hectic with added engagements after their first several performances together. As a duo, they'd skyrocketed to popularity. She sighed and put that memory to rest. That part of her life was over. "What about your husband?" she asked dully. "I knew you were married, but did my father know?"

"Oh, yes." Yvonne's violet eyes flashed a cold hard glance at Joanna's father. "And that was when I discovered how despicable and low your father really is." Keeping her gaze fixed on him, she explained, "My husband never knew my daughter wasn't his. You see, when I first learned I was pregnant, Paul, my husband, was involved in a skiing accident which left him partially paralyzed. Naturally, I couldn't seek a divorce. It would have been the epitome of cruelty. But your father forewarned Steven that, should he have a change of heart about their agreement, he would go to Paul with the blood type reports and tell him the truth. That would have destroyed Paul completely."

Joanna shifted her eyes away from the woman momentarily to shoot a hard gaze at her father. "Lies, Joanna," he rasped. "All lies. The woman's mad!"

Joanna turned away from him and asked Yvonne, "How did this house become yours?"

"It was always mine," Yvonne said, heaving a sigh. "Like I said before, Steven was in financial difficulty, so I leased this house to him when he married you."

Joanna looked puzzled. "I thought you said that Father paid him–"

"The money was paid to Steven *after* your marriage took place," she cut in. "It was only later that Carlton discovered that I held the deed to this house. So, the day after Steven's funeral, when you thought your father was giving a lecture at the university, he was actually confronting me in my home in Los Angeles to demand that I sell this house to him, so that he could turn it over to you, and you would never be the wiser. At the time, I was completely devastated over the death of both Steven *and* my daughter. To be rid of him, I agreed. However, since that time, I changed my mind. I was planning to notify your father about it, but–"

"Say no more, please," Joanna pleaded dryly. She crossed the floor to where her father was standing and stopped just inches before him. She glared at him, waiting for him to once again deny everything, but he could say nothing to defend himself. She broke the silence in a cold tone. "There are no words to express the contempt I feel toward you at this moment. It pains me to wonder what really happened to my mother and Nick's father. But given your despicable nature and your penchant for faking drug-induced heart attacks, I can only hazard a guess that you were directly responsible for both their deaths."

In desperation, he clutched her by the shoulders, digging in with his long, hard fingers. She winced from the pain as he roared, "For God's sake, Joanna, let me explain! I only did it for you! All of it!"

"Stop it! Stop lying to me!" She struggled to free herself from his iron grip. "Let me go! You're hurting me!" she yelled, trying to push him away, but he wouldn't relinquish his hold on her.

Yvonne Martell rushed to her side and grabbed

her father's nearest hand, trying to pry him loose. Just when Joanna thought she was going to faint from the excruciating pain, William appeared as if from nowhere and circled his arm around her father's throat, pulling him away. He tore loose from William and pompously straightened his clothing.

Rubbing her shoulders, Joanna glared at him and announced through gritted teeth, "May God forgive you for the suffering you've brought to everyone you have ever known – because I never will. You're dead to me."

His mouth dropped open. For once, he was speechless.

With eyes full of tears, she cast a pleading glance at William and asked, "Would you kindly take me to the airport?"

William's brows drew downward, and his eyes went to Yvonne Martell as she rushed to Joanna's side. "Joanna, I know this is all difficult for you to accept, and I also know you blamed Steven for everything. But surely you realize now why he was so angry."

Joanna nodded her head as new tears sprang forth. She understood what it felt like to be trapped in a situation she wanted no part of. Steven must have felt the same way, and most of his anger was directed toward her because she was, indirectly, the source and the cause of his predicament. But she was also the reason he enjoyed a resurgence in his career. And still he gave her no quarter. She shook her head free of those confusing thoughts. All of it – *all of it* – was her father's fault. The only thing left for her to do was walk away from him and start living her life with Nick. "Please, William, I need to go back home to the man I love. Take me to the airport, please. Right now."

"B-But Mrs. D.," William protested, "what about the awards ceremony tomorrow night?"

Joanna embraced Yvonne briefly. "I think it is only proper that Mrs. Martell accept the award for Steven." She eyed William. "Now, please, will you take me to the airport?" As William nodded, Joanna swiftly left the room and headed for the foyer.

"Joanna," her father bellowed after her. "Don't leave. Please!"

She ignored him and headed out the door, toward the car still parked in front of the house.

"Joanna!" he yelled again, hurrying to the front entrance. "Wait!"

Reaching for the car door, she turned and considered the man skittering down the steps toward her. She'd called him 'Father' all her life. Only now did she realize he was no father – he was a monster.

"Please," he said, clutching his chest as he breathed laboriously. "My heart can't take this!"

"You have no heart!" she announced. Turning her back on him, she opened the car door, slid into the seat, and slammed the door shut.

CHAPTER TEN

$\mathscr{T}$he taxi slowed to a halt at the entrance to Nick's apartment building. Joanna hurried inside and entered the elevator. After the confrontation with her father and the long flight home, she expected to be spent, but knowing Nick was waiting for her, she felt a rush of urgency and couldn't wait for the elevator doors to open. The next thing she knew, Nick's arms, like bands of steel, pressed her tightly against his naked chest. He mashed his mouth hard against hers and then whispered, "I'm never letting you go again. Never!" He kissed her again ferociously, and she responded by wrapping her arms around his neck, reveling in his sweet abuse. Finally he lifted his head. "Come inside and relax. I can see the exhaustion in your eyes."

It took some effort, but she pulled away from him and walked into the room, tossing her coat, purse, and carryon bag onto the nearest chair. She sighed deeply as she sank down into the couch, then let her gaze settle on Nick. Naked to the waist, he was clad only in tight-fitting jeans that accentuated the broad, taut muscles of his thighs. His dark wavy hair tumbled casually over his brow, and he needed a shave, yet Joanna thought he never looked more handsome. Her pulse raced as she visually devoured him. "You don't know how glad I am to see you again. God, I can't believe it's finally over!"

"Drink this," he suggested, offering her a brandy as he sat down on the couch beside her and draped an arm across her shoulders. "How are you doing?"

"My mind is still trying to process everything that happened today." She gulped the brandy, and it burned pleasantly all the way to her stomach. Running a hand roughly through her hair, she looked sidelong at him. "Aren't you going to say I told you so?"

"No," he said softly. "You've been through enough already, and I'm not going to add to it. You had to find out the truth yourself. I'm just glad you did. The fact is, I feel a sense of responsibility for what happened – to a point."

Joanna looked puzzled. "How do you mean?"

"It's because of me that your father went to such extremes. He hated me and everything I represented. I'm not condoning him for what he did, but I can see how he was driven to do the things he did. If I were in his shoes..." He shrugged. "I might have done the same thing. The man wanted the best for you, and at the time, he believed it was Dalton."

"Bull!" she spat. "He just wanted me as far away from you as possible." Her eyes fell to the fullness of his lower lip, and she sputtered, "I-I'm so very sorry for everything I've put you through."

Lucille Naroian

His dark, thick lashes veiled his glazed eyes, and she guessed he was searching for the right words to comfort her. Finally he spoke, and his voice was thick with passion. "Come here, sweetheart."

A sigh of relief escaped her, and she set her drink aside, then wrapped her arms tightly around his neck. When his mouth eagerly took hers, she gave herself wholly to him. "Nick ... Nick," she groaned, clutching feverishly to him. She was so caught up in the nearness of him, she barely felt his fingers draw apart the buttons on her blouse. He pressed his mouth into the deep hollow of her throat, sending tremors of desire racing through her. She pressed herself closer to him, gasping with a surge of pleasure when his lips caressed the soft fullness of her breasts. She closed her eyes, raking her fingers through his thick mane. Groaning audibly, she wanted the sensations his lips were causing to go on forever.

"Marry me," he murmured. "The sooner the better." He pressed his face into the scented valley of her breasts, and she breathed a sigh of elated contentment as her head swam with the realization ... they were finally free to love and live the rest of their lives together.

~ABOUT THE AUTHOR~

Lucille Naroian lives in northern Massachusetts, and has held a variety of job positions, including chiropractor's assistant, pharmacy technician, and administrator in the stock market. In addition to indulging her love of writing, Lucille is an award-winning portrait artist and enjoys tending her aquarium of tropical fish.

Lucille's debut novel, *Talk of the Town,* is a spicy and humorous romance. *Unforgettable* is her second published novel, an emotional and humorous romance. Look for Lucille's books in ebook and print at Amazon and other popular retailers.

To learn more about Lucille and her books, visit her web site at *www.LucilleNaroian.com*

Unforgettable

by

Lucille Narcian

CHAPTER ONE

Had Maddie Price been paying attention to her surroundings instead of driving recklessly at night in hot pursuit of Alex Bradford, she would have seen the caution lights on the side of the road, slowed down, and avoided the accident. But at that particular moment, Maddie was oblivious to everything. Not even the rain that fell in sheets was capable of putting a halt to her seemingly impossible quest. Therefore, when her Chevy's left front tire slammed into the crater-size pothole and blew out, Maddie was totally unprepared.

Instinctively she hit the brakes, sending the vehicle skidding across the washed-out double lane highway. For a spine-tingling minute, the car spun out of control, then stopped on the muddy shoulder of the road.

When the erratic pounding of her heart finally quieted, she turned off the ignition and gave the steering wheel a frustrated whack.

"Damn you, Alex! It's all your fault!" she yelled, blaming him for causing another catastrophe to come her way. Truth was, she was solely to blame for this mess. Hell-bent on reaching him, she defiantly set out from Boston to Provincetown in a blustering rain storm that was rapidly sweeping up the Eastern seacoast. Fully aware that the major arteries leading south to Cape Cod were flooded, she unwisely disregarded the weatherman's warning to keep off the roads.

Under ordinary circumstances, Maddie would have waited. But time was not on her side. It was imperative she reach Alex tonight ... before dawn ... before he boarded that plane to Paris.

Just thinking about it brought a lump to Maddie's throat. *I can't let that happen*, she told herself, her fury mounting.

With a determined hand, she twisted the key in the ignition and willed the car to move. When the battered tire thumped and sank deeper into the mud, Maddie let out a defeated sob. What was she going to do now? There wasn't a gas station in sight, and even though she wasn't marooned on some desolate road, at this particular stretch she couldn't see any signs of civilization.

Slumping down into the seat, she tried to relax and come up with a viable solution. That's when she remembered catching a glimpse, a few minutes earlier, of a large beach house on the right. Its stately elegance had somehow caught her eye, and she'd noticed, through the rivulets streaming down the side window, a faint ray of light filtering from one of its windows.

A wave of relief swept over her. Someone was nearby. Hope was not lost after all.

She tucked the tapered legs of her jeans into her brown leather boots, and decided to walk back to the house, ignoring the fact that such a trek could put her into a situation more perilous than the one she was in now. Nevertheless, it was a chance she had to take.

With her purse tucked under her arm, she reached for the door handle. Just as she touched it, a jagged streak of lightning split the sky. A violent gust of wind rocked her small car. Terror gripped her as she waited for the car to still. When it finally did, she reconsidered the danger and abandoned her attempt to seek help.

Gazing forlornly out the rain-drenched window, she considered her options. Not a soul had passed by since she'd been there, and it was doubtful that anyone would. Therefore, option one was to stay put and wait out the storm. Mulling it over, she decided that choice was out of the question. The idea of spending the night in an impotent vehicle sent shivers along her spine.

What if the storm developed into a hurricane? She'd have no chance of survival in her old Chevy. The car was too lightweight to guarantee her safety. Therefore, option two was her only choice. She'd have to change the tire herself. It didn't matter that she'd never attempted to change a tire before. The fact was, it had to be done.

Resigned to her fate, she took a deep breath and accepted the challenge. With a not-so-steady hand, she removed the key from the ignition, tied a silk scarf around her coiled, honey blond hair, and turned up the collar on her navy pea jacket.

Moving quickly, she reached over to the glove compartment and withdrew a dented yellow flashlight. She couldn't remember the last time she'd used the old thing, and was certain that by now the batteries were dead. Holding her breath, she switched it on. A bright beam of light spread across the seat. She smiled. Something had finally gone right. She switched off the light, pushed open the door, and carefully stepped out.

To her horror, the water on the road reached to the top of her boots. Worse yet, the pothole had practically swallowed the useless tire completely. Emitting a groan, she squinted her eyes against the driving rain and crouched down beside the fender to inspect the damage, wondering how she was going to wedge a jack under a bumper she could barely see, and in sloppy mud where solid ground should be. Her worries went into overdrive. *What if the damage went beyond the tire? What if the axle or frame was broken?* If that were the case, she'd have to total the car, because the cost of repairs would far exceed what the old clunker was worth.

Suddenly, Maddie shook her head and stood upright, refusing to give in to another negative thought. It was simply tire trouble, she told herself, and nothing more. And if she was ever going to reach Alex tonight, she'd better get moving.

Pulling the jacket collar tighter around her neck, she turned and waded to the rear of the car. Just as she reached the trunk, she heard a sound. Hesitating a moment, she scanned the washed-out road, the stretch of isolated beach, then the sides and rear of the car, but saw nothing. Her imagination was playing tricks on her, she decided, as she shrugged her shoulders and slid the trunk key into the lock.

As soon as the lock clicked, she heard that sound again. Switching on the flashlight, she aimed it in the direction of the noise. What she saw turned her insides to jelly.

Coming at her with lightning speed was the largest Doberman Pinscher she had ever seen. Black as the night, it charged through the murky water, its glassy eyes and sharp pointed teeth well illuminated by the lightning.

Unable to move, Maddie heard a sob leave her

throat, and her knees went weak as she realized in a moment she would become the victim of this deadly creature.

With only the thin flashlight for protection, she clutched it tightly, crossed her arms against her chest, and dug her chin deep into her jacket collar. It was all just too much! Standing beside a useless hunk of junk with that hellhound charging toward her, she vowed that if she lived through this, she would get even with Alex one way or another.

The dog, just inches away, focused its eyes intently on her. When she heard the beast's low, throaty growl, she flung the flashlight in its path and somehow found the strength to run. It was a mistake she soon regretted. As if fired from a cannon, the dog shot up on its hind legs and pounced, pinning Maddie's shoulders to the side of the car with its huge paws. She could actually feel the heat of its breath on her throat as it opened its jaws wider.

A wave of dizziness came over her and, for a moment, she prayed she *would* faint. Unable to face her fate with the attack-dog snarling at her throat, she shut her eyes tight. Her only thought now was that she didn't want to die ... *not here* ... *not like this*.

What Maddie needed was a miracle, and it came just in time, in the form a pickup truck that screeched to a halt beside her. Because of the howling wind, she didn't hear the driver's door slam, but she did hear a piercing whistle, and that's when her eyes flew open. The animal responded immediately to the sound and mercifully slid its heavy claw-tipped paws from Maddie's trembling shoulders. Immediately she felt a different pressure replacing the dog's paws – a pair of strong, yet comforting hands.

Maddie lifted her gaze to meet the stranger's shadowed face. When he spoke, his voice was gentle with seeming genuine concern. "Are you hurt?"

"N-no," she stammered with a sigh of relief as she wiped the stream of tears and rain from her eyes. "B-but the dog. Please get him away from me!"

The stranger pulled the hood of his slicker further down to shield his face from the pounding rain. "Don't be afraid, miss!" he shouted. "He belongs to me. I'm real sorry he frightened you."

Immediately anger replaced her fear. "Frighten me!" she snapped. "He was ready to tear out my throat! How dare you let something like that run loose? He belongs on a leash. Better yet, in a cage!"

The man stiffened. "I never let Caesar run loose. He got away from me when I went outside to lock the gate. Hard to believe, but he's never done this before. He must have sensed there was trouble up the road, and apparently he was right." The man reached down and patted the dog, who now stood still beside his master. Turning, the animal jumped onto the open back of the truck.

The man took a step backwards, reached into the pocket of his slicker, and took out a long silver flashlight. Switching it on, he gave the Chevy the once over. "What's wrong with your car?"

Maddie's shoulders sagged, both from embarrassment and utter helplessness. "I'm afraid I wasn't paying attention and hit something in the road!" she shouted, trying to be heard above the wind. "It ruined my tire."

"Must have been that damn pothole!" he shouted back. "Didn't you see the warning sign?"

"What warning sign?"

"Back there, on that pole," he answered, pointing behind him. "There's a sign and a set of bright yellow caution lights. Even in this rain, you couldn't have missed them."

She could barely make out what he was saying as he waded off to inspect the battered tire. Centering the light on the tattered wheel, he remarked, "You must have been going like a bat out of hell!"

"Never mind that!" she snapped. "The important thing is, can you fix it for me? I have a spare in the trunk."

He turned the flashlight on her angry face. "No way, miss."

"Please, mister," she begged. "I just have to get to Provincetown tonight!"

The stranger switched off the light and returned it to his pocket. "The tire's wedged too deeply in the mud. Looks like your car is going to have to sit here until the storm ends."

"I can't wait that long!" she shouted, blinking her eyes rapidly against the rain. "Didn't you hear me? I've got to get there *tonight!*"

The man became impatient. "I heard you perfectly, miss, but again, I can't help you. Not tonight, anyway."

Maddie sighed and thought a minute. "What about a gas station? Isn't there one around here somewhere?"

"Sure," he yelled. "There's one just around the bend. But it's closed because of the storm. Sorry, but you're just going to have to wait till tomorrow."

She gasped. "Tomorrow's too late!" Balling her fists in frustration, she turned quickly and began trudging towards the driver's side of the car.

The stranger caught her by the arm. "Why is tomorrow too late?" he asked. "Is there a family emergency?"

"No, there's no family emergency," she replied harshly. She was not about to admit she had risked life and limb in a futile attempt to stop a man from leaving her. She turned her face away and frowned. "I'll just stay here for the night."

The man eyed her closely and said in disbelief, "You don't really plan to spend the night in this wreck!"

"Yes, I do." She felt absolutely sick inside.

"That's crazy!" he said, his patience obviously wearing thin. "My place is about three hundred yards back down the road. You're welcome to stay the night. It's better than being alone out here. At least you'll be dry ... and safe."

And safe. It was strange the way he had tagged on that last phrase. She understood he had paused purposely for effect.

As if capable of reading her thoughts, the man gave her a reassuring smile. "Look, I can understand your apprehension. If I were a woman in this predicament, I'd be leery of going off with a stranger myself. But, it's your choice."

Looking up at him, Maddie replied in an equally placating tone, "Thanks. I appreciate the offer."

He gave her a quick smile. "So, what do you say? And make it quick before we both catch pneumonia."

No sooner had he asked the question when a streak of lightning struck a tree stump on the opposite side of the road, splitting it in two. It was all Maddie needed. "Yes!"

* * * * *

Settling herself beside the stranger in his warm truck, Maddie got a closer look at him as he pushed back the hood on his slicker and threaded long fingers through his thick, dark hair. The sight of his handsome profile etched against the intermittent flashes of lightning brought an unexpected flush to her cheeks. She pressed her icy cold palms against her face, hoping he hadn't noticed, but he had.

Patting her gently on her arm, he said reassuringly, "Relax. Everything will turn out okay." Maddie knew he was trying to banish her fear. But what she was feeling was anything *but* fear. Sitting there, so close to him, she felt the flutter of butterflies in the pit of her stomach. Swallowing hard, she managed to lie with some degree of conviction. "I'm not nervous. Just hot one minute, cold the next."

"A shot of brandy will take care of that," he replied as he moved his hand and started the engine.

Confused by her emotional response to his nearness and touch, Maddie sat back and tried to relax, but when she glanced at her disabled car, she became deeply depressed. Even if the storm ended by dawn as expected, and she was able to get help from one of the garages in town, it would be too late to reach Alex. Tears of despair brimmed in her eyes; she shut them tightly to hold them back. She remained lost in her melancholy until the stranger stopped the truck and turned off the engine.

Opening her eyes, she peered out the windshield and grinned, thinking it ironic that this rambling house was the one she'd thought of trying to reach earlier.

After pulling the hood back over his head, Maddie's companion got out of the truck, then closing the door behind him, summoning his dog with a loud whistle. Fast on his master's heels, the beast began running in circles, visibly happy to be home.

Odd, but Maddie felt the same as she followed closely behind and inspected the front exterior of the house. Flanking the crushed seashell driveway sat a low stone wall shrouded with storm-driven leaves from the belt of trees that formed a semi-circle around the house. Wide brick steps led to a white oversized paneled door. Centered between the panels was a brass plate on which the name Kendall was inscribed.

Maddie turned to him and asked, "Are you *Mr.* Kendall?"

"In the flesh," he quipped. "But please, call me Robert. And you?"

"Madelyn Price," she answered softly. "But everyone calls me Maddie."

"Nice to meet you, Maddie. Welcome to my humble abode."

Robert inserted the key in the lock, then thrust open the door and gestured Maddie inside. When all three had entered the narrow foyer, the dog placed himself in front of her, gave a low, throaty growl, and raised his proud head in protest to her admittance. Continuing to growl, he bared his sharp, white teeth. Instinctively Maddie jumped back and brought the heel of her boot firmly down on the toe of Robert's boot. When he let out a painful howl, Maddie quickly jumped forward. Pivoting around, she came face to face with the tall, handsome Robert Kendall.

Although the foyer was dimly lit, they could

clearly see each other's face. For a moment, their eyes met and locked, sending a disquieting shiver racing through Maddie's already drenched and shivering body. Finally, she came to her senses. "E-excuse me," she stammered, blushing profusely.

"No harm done." He smiled, gazing down at her face as he removed his rain-streaked slicker. He then held out his hand for her jacket and scarf. Caesar continued to growl in protest. This time Robert turned to the dog and commanded, "Enough!" Maddie was impressed to find that one word was all it took to quiet the animal, who turned and sauntered towards the fireplace.

Grateful to be rid of her sopping wet coverings, Maddie quickly handed them to Robert, who draped them over a ladder-back chair near the fire.

Stepping quickly to the closet in the hall, Robert opened the door and deposited his slicker inside. After closing it, he placed his hands on his hips and gazed directly into Maddie's wide aquamarine eyes. A smile played gently on his lips. "Now for those wet clothes," he practically whispered, savoring the way her V-neck sweater clung to her full rounded breasts with their peaks pointed straight at him.

Her skin tight jeans were molded to her slim hips and long shapely legs, causing the muscles in his jaw to tighten. *God, she's incredible*, he thought, then mentally shook himself from the direction his mind was taking him.

Maddie stood there like a mannequin, unable to move under his intimate stare, but her mind was racing a mile a minute. She knew what he was thinking, and for some inexplicable reason, she welcomed the intimate gaze. It brought an immediate flush to her cheeks. Suddenly she remembered that they had forgotten her luggage in the trunk of her car.

"My suitcases!" she gasped. "How could I have forgotten them? Everything I–"

"Relax. I'll go back and get them," he said tightly, trying not to reveal his displeasure. Right now, the last thing in the world he wanted to do was take his eyes off her incredible body and trudge back out into the storm. But he had no choice, he told himself. After all, if he was going to play a knight-in-shining-armor, he had to take the bad with the good. Heaving a sigh, he pointed at Maddie and ordered, "Don't move."

Now what? she wondered, wrapping her arms around herself. She was freezing, and he had to know it. So, why wasn't he leading her to the fireplace to warm herself? And where was he going, she wondered, as he went around the fireplace and disappeared.

He was back in seconds, holding a towel and a blue terrycloth robe, which, from the looks of its size, was definitely his, and a pair of terrycloth slippers to match.

"Here, dry off and put these on." He pushed the items into her trembling hands. "You can put your wet things in the dryer in the mud room, which is right across from you. Those jeans will take forever to dry in front of the fire."

Then, like a game show contestant who was trying to beat the clock or lose the prize, he flung open the closet door, grabbed his slicker, and went over to the dog. "You," he snapped at the animal, who looked back at him with a raised eyebrow, "don't you dare move! Understand?"

The dog raised the other brow at the command. His master rarely left the house without him. Caesar's gaze turned to Maddie. So did Robert's.

"Where are your keys?"

"In my purse on the chair. And thank y–"

"No problem," he stated flatly. He opened the purse, grabbed the keys, and slammed the door behind him.

* * * * *

"Nice doggie," Maddie said in a quivering voice, striving to remain calm as she stepped cautiously to the fire. The dog's ominous stare followed her every move, increasing her nervousness. She didn't trust the beast. Not for a minute.

As their eyes locked, she sucked in a deep, unsteady breath and slowly removed her boots. Her heart hammered wildly against her chest as she began to remove her sweater. Even when it dropped to the floor, the dog's eyes never left hers. Becoming increasingly agitated, she wanted to tell the animal to stop looking at her *that* way.

"Now I know why they call dogs man's best friend," she stated, glaring back at him. "Men and dogs relate perfectly. A female is a female whether she has two legs or four."

Still peering at him out of the corner of her eye, she removed the pins from her hair and set them on the mantle. After wiping her face dry with the towel, she pushed her hair forward, then twisted the towel around it turban style.

Praying she'd be in the robe before Robert returned, she quickly unzipped her jeans, hooked her thumbs into the waistbands of both the jeans and panties, and began inching them down her legs.

"You could at least have the decency to turn your head!" she snapped, standing totally naked before the gazing beast.

"Why should he? He has good taste, just like his master."